Protecting Avalon

Lauren Jeffares Parra

ISBN 978-0-692-72683-9

Library of Congress 2016909059

Contents

Prologue

The island winds were steadily blowing the calm sea. The sound of the water moving over the sand was rejuvenating as the salt air rose. It was a cloudy and warm day. The sun would show itself through the clouds every now and then making it truly a perfect day for a walk on the beach. Alick was only a boy of twelve years of age kicking rocks by the shore. Brown shaggy hair, matching eyes, and naturally tanned skin, he was enjoying the beautiful weather, carrying his father's sword, on a break from the ship that was anchored in nearby water. His father had taught him everything he knew, from sword fighting to being loyal and honest. He was young, but intelligent and knew how to mend the sails. He worked as hard as three men and already showed characteristics of a great leader. He was a very brave boy; it seemed nothing ever frightened him. As captain of the ship and a well-known leader, his father had always been hard on him and expected much from him.

This was the first time in weeks they had stopped and Alick had stepped foot on land. This wasn't the longest time he could remember being out at sea, he was used to it and never complained, but, still, he admitted to himself that it was nice to have solid ground beneath him. He walked a little further up the shoreline than he had noticed, towards some high cliffs. The ship was just out of sight when he saw her for the first time. Just over the rocks was a girl, the most beautiful girl he had ever seen. The light was gleaming down on her. She had long blonde hair which carried a flower crown tangled in it. Her purple dress was made out of silk. She was picking up some sea shells when he suddenly came up on her and startled her.

"Don't be afraid, my name is Alick."

"I am called Irena," she responded keeping her distance. 'Irena' he thought, 'what an enchanting name.' They had paused lingering in the moment without breaking their gaze. It was only a few seconds, but to Alick it felt as if time had stood still. The trance was broken by a man's voice. Off in the distance behind her must have been over fifty ships anchored down near the shoreline, and a man on the shore was yelling for her to come.

"I must go."

"Wait!" Alick said. She stopped, "here." He handed her a large sea shell that he was standing over, "For your collection." She thanked him and ran off towards the man that had been calling to her. Alick watched from afar as she ran down and jumped into the man's arms. He assumed it was her father, still wrapped in amazement by the pretty girl named Irena and more ships than he had ever seen together at once, or at least than he could count, he quickly turned and headed back.

Alick hurried to place the sword back into his father's room where he had found it before his father discovered it was missing. Just as he turned, his father walked in.

"Father, there are over fifty ships on the other side of the cliff going east. I saw them," Alick said with excitement.

"Yes, Alick, there are several different countries uniting for a feast with the king tomorrow night. My boy, I didn't want to tell you this and worry you until I knew for sure, but we are headed for the city of Avalon where King Theron is preparing for war, and we are fighting as his allies."

"You should have told me Papa, I am ready to fight with you."

"No my son, I have other plans in mind for you, but we shall discuss these things after we arrive. Help the men on deck to set sail, please."

"Yes, father." The plan was to arrive into the city before night fall. All the other ships had a head start.

"Let's catch up quick, shall we, and show the others what this vessel can do?" Alick left the room with astonishment, and his father gazed at the sword lying in the room, crooked from where he had left it. After a quick smirk he sat down to rest from a long day's work, and his eyes settled on the familiar drawing of Alick's mother underneath a dim lantern on the cupboard beside his bed.

PART 1

1. Avalon

When we arrived to Avalon, the city was chaos. People from all around the world were coming off different ships and standing all around us. Hundreds were running back and forth with hands full, some shoving to get through the crowd. I could remember being here once before, two years ago when I was a younger child, although, this time I noticed more detail, like the immense size of the city. Everything seemed different from what I could remember, except the smell, I hadn't forgotten the smell, and it was the same, full of fresh trees and tropical flowers. I can still remember every detail of that very short weekend so incredibly well. Avalon was now growing immensely with people from across the globe. There was still the

Baker's shop in the market, which was owned by an old family friend. It was the most popular store, known for its delicious bread. But there was much more set up in the market this time with many tents alongside the streets selling meats, which was mostly fish caught from off the coast. There was one particular tent that I stopped to look at. I purchased a unique compass. My father and I collected such trinkets. As I wandered further along the city, I noticed that most of Avalon was made up of marble or stone. Vines grew over the walls and sides and reminded me of a jungle. The city was the largest I had ever seen, and very easy to get lost in, almost like a maze. There were beautiful white columns holding the city together in many main entrance-ways. I had never seen so many strange plants before, but then again I was never on land long enough to discover much of anything new. Music lifted into the air to settle the anxiety of war. The women and children went home to bed while the men went out into the night to speak of the plans for battle. My father never explained much of war to me. And I was only a child then, but I can still remember everything that transpired over those next few days as if it had happened only yesterday. Those days were the start of my beginning, my purpose, and soon would become a nightmare that would haunt me for the rest of my life.

From what I could learn, our rivals were fierce and to be feared upon. We were told to never underestimate the enemy. We had heard they consisted of large numbers greater than our own, yet that was hard for me to believe, for our own army contained thousands of men from many countries. Our enemy was also known to be evil. They wanted to take everything from us and kill the people without any cause. Their leader was named Damion. People hesitated to mention his name, but I heard of him at times during the first day at port in hushed whispers. You had to either join his army or be killed. I heard rumors he would do anything to take over the city and become the new king. He wanted control and power over everything and everyone. He had never lost at battle thus far, so we needed to keep his army from reaching the gates or it would mean sure defeat.

Strange things began to happen to me on this trip; I was beginning to learn things about my family. Along with rumors of war, there were also secrets of the royal family I had overheard from gossips of strangers in the market on several different occasions, but rarely paid attention to that sort of thing. If something odd stuck out to me, I then listened carefully to the conversations that interested me. I'm sure I learned certain things I probably wasn't meant to hear. I proved to be very observant. My father kept silent on most matters concerning war. However, he did have news for me the night before battle, but nothing would ever prepare me for the words he would soon speak to me and what they would truly mean.

During the next day, which was my first full day in this city filled with wonder, while everyone planned for attack, I went to discover some sort of adventure for myself. I wandered aimlessly, not finding much amusement, and happened upon a group of boys. They were all about my age and became aggressive with me, as I accidently found them out in an act of mischief. I wasn't frightened. They were all scrawny, except the leader of their group, Cadman. He was a lot younger than me, but built just as tall. A guard noticed the boys picking a fight and sent me on my way before things became too heated. Just as well – I needed to be on my way.

That night held the dinner my father had been speaking about ever since we had arrived. It was the ceremonial feast of the night before war would begin, and my father would be honored as a guest of the king. The food was delicious. There were many types of food served on the table in front of me. I can still almost taste and smell the divine foods of that night. That entire event seemed so magical. Every person in the room was wearing jewels and riches of every color that fit them all like a puzzle piece. I had met so many people in just the two days since we had arrived and had already made many friends, most of which were adults. People often remarked that I had an old soul. I could carry a conversation with anyone. We were never in a place too long and it was hard for me to get close with anyone, so I usually kept to myself. Besides, in my head, I had this idea that people looked at me as some sort of a mystery. In a way I liked it.

Not even ten minutes into conversation the horns blew to invite everyone who was sitting to rise so that the queen and princess could be announced. When they made their entrance, people bowed, and I nearly fell over when I noticed the little girl from the first day on the beach standing beside the queen. She was just as beautiful, if not even more than when I saw her for the second time. This time she was wearing a green silk dress, and I suddenly couldn't believe my eyes. She was wearing a seashell necklace with pearls, and attached in the very center was the large sea shell I had found and given to her. I had heard talk earlier in the day that it was the princess's tenth birthday. We all sat to start eating again, but I couldn't keep myself from constantly glancing her way. She noticed me as well and blushed slightly it seemed when our eyes met.

After dinner, the husband's danced with their wives as if they would never stop. It could have been their last night together. It's as if that night everything stood still and no one cared for tomorrow. Guards had previously prepared armory, weapons, and final strategies, which were ready for battle the next day, so everyone could enjoy the night together without worries. The king planned it all this way in advance because he believed in love and family before anything else, just as my father did. This night was a celebration for all. Eventually, father took me up to meet the King and Queen and, after bowing, introduced me to Irena.

"Hello again," I said.

"You two know each other?" My father asked.

"Yes we met at the beach," said Irena.

"Very interesting," said the King as he looked over to my father.

"Irena darling, why don't you entertain our guest with a dance so your father can talk about plans for tomorrow," suggested the Queen Isadora.

We walked to the center of the floor and seemed to have gained quite an audience in the room, as it grew quieter and a space cleared out for us to dance. A few were whispering. I hadn't the slightest idea why? Was someone like me not supposed to dance with a princess? Was I dancing wrong? I had never danced before, but it looked easy enough from watching the crowd earlier. Cadman and his group made sure to give me faces of contempt, but I noticed their expressions shift as they looked upon Irena. She was so graceful and pretty; I didn't really know what to say. I felt like I had always known her somehow. There was an odd feeling when we touched; it's hard to find the words - almost like a spark that had shocked us both. It felt right. We didn't speak much, but I knew we were communicating deeper, as if we knew each other's thoughts.

"I like your necklace," It was the only thing that would surface.

"Thank you, a nice boy gave it to me, I like it better than all my other gifts." She made me smile for an instant before I asked, "What do you know of this war?"   She frowned, "he is coming for me."

I was confused, "Who?" She was quiet. When she spoke, she asked me why no one had told me. "Told me what?"

"I shouldn't speak of it," she replied. Just then, King Theron interrupted us to dance with his daughter. "Of course," I said and gave her off with a bow. I had so many questions. I wanted to know what Princess Irena was talking about. None of it made sense.

Later, I found my father in his chamber waiting for me; it was like he had been expecting me to seek him.

"My boy, please come in, I have many things I wish to speak with you about, and we don't have very much time."

"Father, what is this war really about?" I asked. He stared at me for quite a while and finally spoke, "There is something you need to understand. I think you are old enough to know the truth." He paused for a second and then continued, "Princess Irena is immortal as long as she stays alive and well then she will live forever, and she is the only one who can defeat Damion's power."

"That's not possible!"

"Indeed it is. And that is only just the beginning. I have so much to tell you, so please listen closely. I wish I had more time and you were much older. I knew this day would come eventually, but I never imagined it to come so soon." My father paused for a few seconds and then began again. "Nothing I am about to tell you can prepare you for your journey ahead. Irena has powers of her own. Damion and any other evil in the world will always come to find her and use her for themselves. This world is selfish and has become wicked in sin. You are meant to stay by her side and protect her until she is old enough and ready to face and defeat Damion. I really wish I had more time to prepare you for all of this."

"Father it sounds like you've had too much to drink. You sound crazy, are you ill?" With an amused huff my father leaned over and looked me straight in the eyes and said, "I'm being serious with you, and there's more. I always knew you were different from other children. The birthmark you have on your shoulder means, 'new beginning.' " I had to sit down, I still wasn't completely convinced he wasn't drunk, but I dared not mentioning it again. I knew to never question my father. I did have a distinct mark on my shoulder with a line of freckles that looked like a constellation form of the Orion stars. My father had always teased me about it and had prophets examine me, never telling me what they had told him. I thought he was teasing me again, but surely my father wouldn't joke at a time like this.

"Princess Irena has power, and she will live forever as a young woman unless she is hurt or killed. When you were born and your mother died I suppose you were blessed. Many believed the signs that you were immortal as well. There is a prophecy that there will be a man who will protect mankind forever. We believe it is you. That is what your mark means. It is why we named you Alick, which also means 'protector of mankind.' If you die you will be born again. It is unsure if you will have the same body or if you will even remember who you are. I'm not completely convinced this is your first life; you have such an old soul. I think you are an ancient warrior at heart." I didn't know what to say, I didn't believe him. And if he were telling me the truth, why had I not heard of these things before now? How come the princess knew about it before me? I was trying to take it all in and then I asked the most important question, "If Irena is the only one who can defeat Damion, why would you go to battle? If you know we can't win?"

"I must fight with the King and try my best to destroy his army. The odds are against us, but we are only trying to keep the people safe and deter him from Irena for more time. She isn't ready to face him yet; she is too young and not strong enough. Damion wants her. Irena's power is said to be capable of keeping another who she is closest to forever young as well. He wants to hold her prisoner for eternity, so he can live forever. He seeks power and wants to be the most powerful person in the world. You must not speak of this to anyone, or she will have more than one enemy coming after her." He explained all that he could to me, the best he could. Very few people in the city knew of her powers and were sworn to secrecy, ready to defend the princess. My head spun; this was all too much information to take in for one night. "Son, do not be afraid. Use everything I have taught you. This is your destiny, to keep the people of Avalon safe and to protect Irena. Your mother was from this city, so these are your people, too. If anything goes wrong, evacuate as many people possible and head northeast, where you will find safety. You know we have many allies; you have seen them and been to most of the places for yourself. You are smart, and I believe in you. Above all else, always protect Irena." My father handed me his sword. He had always carried this sword ever since I could remember. It was his father's sword before him. "Promise me son, keep her safe, for she is our only hope for the future." I agreed, not sure of what else to say, "Yes I will," I replied. "I promise." I knew this was important to him, so I accepted what responsibility would come.

      "Good, now get some rest; tomorrow will be a long day for us all. 'How was I supposed to sleep now,' I thought? All of his words spun recklessly in my mind, making my head throb. I wondered about my immortality and how it could be so – whether a blessing or a curse. Do I really want to live forever? I didn't know exactly how I felt about it, but I was exhausted and needed to sleep on it. I closed my eyes and slowly was taken from altered reality by sleep. I dreamed of Irena standing on the beach. I would awake from nightmares, thinking Irena was taken. In my tossing and turning, I began to question whether the conversation with my father was just a dream. Whether awake or asleep nothing seemed real. My father had always spoken the truth. I know better than to doubt the man, and, even if I wasn't convinced, if this was what he asked of me, I would try my hardest to keep everyone safe. Since I wasn't able to fight along my father's side, it was the least I could do.

The next morning I awoke early without hearing of my father's departure. I went for a walk to clear my head from the night's troubles. The people of Avalon were putting on their armor, grabbing weapons, and saying their good byes. I went walking around the highest towers so I could have a good look of everything happening down below. I heard someone whisper for me, and when I turned, princess Irena signaled for me from a doorway. I wasn't much in the mood for conversation and was a little frustrated with her for reasons I couldn't understand. It was probably more because I had to stay there instead of go to battle. But also, because she was a younger girl, who knew of everything before I did, which didn't seem right nor fair.

"I must show you the passage ways in case we must escape." We talked a few moments about where all the passages would lead. And then I asked her, "Do you want to be immortal? Do you really believe it? How do you feel knowing you are the only one who can stop this dark army?"

She replied, "I guess your father finally told you. What we have is a gift, we were chosen for this."

"I didn't ask for this!" I couldn't help myself from arguing.

"No, you didn't, but I have faith in you. I knew when I saw you sitting with your father last night that the prophecy was true." I looked at her with a confused face. I wasn't aware of the prophecy. "Because we had met at the beach, earlier, before we had really known one another," she kept explaining.

"What does that have to do with anything?" I asked, still confused.

"You are destined to protect me, our people, and some day, when I'm ready, I am destined to face Damion and defeat him. And we are also destined by fate to always find one other. We found each other that day on the beach, that's how I know it's true."

"Is there anything else I should know about?" I asked.

"The fact that we were alone on the beach by chance is rare; I am almost never left alone. I only walked by myself that day because it was my birthday wish and father let me go by my own request." She continued, "that is all for now, I must go find my father before he leaves and you should go and find yours also. We have some goodbyes to say, just in case." She held her head down as she left, and I started running for the port, taking in everything she had just said. She seemed wise for such a young girl and somehow accepted everything much better than I was able to.

The ships had been made ready, and the sun was starting to rise over the water. This was the day. I could feel the change coming in the wind. The King thanked me for watching over his daughter and told me I was now in charge while he was away. I gave my father one last hug, as I knew it would probably be the last time I would ever see him, and tears fell from my eyes.

"I love you, my son. I may not have said it enough. Remember your promise to me; keep it always. Your mother would be so proud of you. This is my place where I belong; always remember where you belong."

"I Promise, I Promise," I kept whispering as he walked further away from me, "I Promise, I Promise." I then watched my father and the thousands of brave men sail into the deep ocean waters.

We waited in the high towers and watched the ships sail into battle. It was too far away for us to see what was happening, but there were other ships with messengers to bring first news of any change. The ships looked like little specs over the horizon. We could barely make out the dark enemy sails in the distance. There were many, far more than our own. I imagined I could hear the yells and battle screams of multiple men. The hope was that we would kill off most of his army, and they would turn around and give up. There were guards posted at the gates down below, should any enemy get past the waters onto land and start moving towards the city. There were archers surrounding the castle walls ready to attack. Irena and her mother went inside. They did not care to remain as the first canon sounds were making their way to our ears. I sat with Emeth who was an older man. He was the King's trusted advisor for many years and also an old friend of my father. Should anything ever happen to the king, he swore an oath to stay alongside the princess and help her to make the best decisions for her country. He was very wise and loyal. I finally had time to meet and speak with him. Given the circumstances, it was nice to be distracted. That's when I learned that Cadman was his son. He was a very tough boy, almost nine years of age, with bright blonde hair and dark skin. He was popular with everyone around our age. He always seemed to play around and pick on others, just looking for trouble if you asked me. The battle went on for hours, and it started to rain outside, making it tough to see. I was very inpatient waiting for any sort of news, until finally we saw a few boats heading our way. It didn't look good. The men were yelling something toward the port and there were enemy sails following close behind. I ran toward the beach as fast as I could before Emeth tried to stop me, but I threw him aside. He was still calling out to me when I reached the cobblestone street, but I never turned or hesitated. I yelled for them to hurry and open the gates for the men and to shut it back before the other ships came. They looked terrified and were out of breath trying to get the words out.

"It's over. There's nothing else we can do!"

"What of my father and the king?" I asked. "Damion has dark magic. Before the battle began he had dark waters render our ships useless. We had no control and could only fight with our swords. Your father was still fighting last we saw. We have killed half of Damion's army, but it is larger than our own. The king is dead. He was captured and killed by Damion himself." 'No! How could this be happening?'

"Someone, please go and spread the news to the Queen and get the others ready to evacuate," said another warrior. I was still in shock and couldn't move.

"I am sorry, boy, about your father," said one of the men who made it back, his hand resting on my shoulder. Suddenly, I broke away and ran toward the tower I had descended. I remembered my promise; I would save as many people as possible. It was all happening too quickly. I didn't feel prepared and never imagined that it could really happen. As soon as I returned to the top and looked, some of the ships were already there, and the enemy was stepping onto land. They had black armor and were running quickly to the gates. The city was in panic, women screaming, children crying, and Queen Isadora had lost herself in grief. I knew I had to do something.

"Everyone come this way, we must leave now!" I yelled. To my surprise, people around me headed to the exit ways I had been shown. "We must hurry. Let's go now!" I told the queen, but she would not listen.

Irena was in tears, "I love you my mother," she said crying.

"I love you my darling," Queen Isadora said back to her, as she let go of Irena's hand. "Keep her safe," the Queen said to me.

"Come on!" She would not listen. "Why isn't the queen coming with us?"

"My mother would never leave our city with the absence of my father. She has powers, too, and can fight them." I didn't want to ask Irena any more questions. We had to go now, and she was upset and looked horrified and pale.

When we reached the end of the passage, it led us out of the back of the city and up through some mountain passages. There were horses prepared and wagons with blankets and food. There were nearly three hundred of us ready to travel. Only the children were allowed to ride in the wagons. We had only about forty horses, so most people were on foot. Some carried excess items that couldn't be strapped to the horses or fit in the buggies. Amongst the group, there were only fifty warriors with weaponry. The rest stayed behind to hold down the castle walls and deter the enemy from following us. My father had told me to ride northeast, and I planned to eventually, but right now we had to get out harm's way and move north. Northeast was a path visible from the beach, we needed to head in the thickness of the forest to disappear. We were headed straight towards some snowy mountains, and I knew it would be a rough journey for us to travel, but we had no other choice. The oceans were congested with the enemy, and our ships were almost all destroyed. Walking was the only way out. We knew it would take another day or two for Damion's army to take over the rest of the city. So after many miles, we set up camp and rested. The people huddled together to mourn the dead king and queen, who was as good as dead. Irena silently left a flower at each grave before returning to her tent. I thought that was good; she needed rest because the next day would be hard. We had a huge head start, but were slow with large numbers on foot, compared to the skilled squadrons of enemy warriors on horseback.

We passed through many villages, mostly consisting of women and children. Some of them joined us from fear of being left alone. Several men kept watch at night in case of an unexpected attack. Irena had kept quiet ever since we escaped and whenever we stopped to rest, she would retreat to her tent until it was again time to move. I sat by the fire and thought of my father. The men had last seen him alive. What if he could still be alive? What if he was being held captive? And what had the queen thought she could do? Surely, she would be killed as well. I know Irena must have been overwhelmed. She had to mourn both of her parents and found herself alone. My emotions drained my body and made me mentally tired. As the guards kept watch I knew I should take the chance to sleep. I was only twelve and had just taken responsibility for a nation. I knew I had a long journey ahead of me. Looking up at the stars, my eyes slowly closed, and I drifted away. I dreamed of being at sea, which is where I loved to be the most. I dreamed of being captain just like my father. My dream seemed so real I could almost taste the salt in the air and hear the waves crashing together and the boards of the ship creaking while the ship rocked. I could feel the ship swaying from side to side. And then I dreamed of a foggy night at sea with the other ships surrounding us. I could hear my father yelling for me to wake up. *Wake up!*

I opened my eyes and it was still dark. I could hear the crickets. One of the warriors was nudging me, telling me to get up. It was again time to move because we needed a good head start so I quickly began packing up my belongings. We extinguished the fire, hoping nobody nearby noticed the smoke. Irena had finally come out of her tent when all but hers were left to be packed. She was riding her father's black stallion. I was riding a horse given to me by Emeth, a tan horse with a white nose and a beautiful brown mane. We had been in deep woods for some time now. The land had started to incline, which made it more difficult for us to pull up the wagons. We had to pass through the mountains before changing the direction of choice. We spent days walking and covering our tracks. It began to get much colder, and we were eventually walking through snow-covered grounds. The women complained as their children cried out, and it was clear that something needed to be done differently. We were running out of food and supplies. It was known that small villages existed throughout the mountain valleys and could offer us shelter. A few men had decided to hunt, and I went along with them. While hunting, we all spoke of another option. We needed to split up our group. Half would take the women and children somewhere warmer, while the rest of us kept moving with the princess to find a large city where she would be protected. This made sense to me, since it was the princess that the enemy was really tracking. Keeping us all together meant endangering the people and slowing the princess.

When we returned to camp we told the people of our plan, and they all agreed unanimously that it should be done. It had been rough for the women, and the children had grown weary. The next day, ten warriors went in one direction with half the horses and a dozen wagons. The remainder of the warriors and a few others including Emeth, Cadman, two servant maids, and I stayed with the princess. After two days we finally made it through the snowy mountains and started northeast like my father had asked of me. Irena still hadn't spoken, so one day while hunting, I found some white flowers that I picked and brought back to her.

"I thought these may brighten up your tent." She smiled.

"Thank you, it is very kind of you to think of me."

"It's nice to see you smile again," I told her.

I wish I could say we finally made it to a safe destination, but traveling became a way of life for us for many years. Every time we found somewhere we thought would be safe, the dark army would soon be upon us. These were dark times. We were on the run, sadly, for more days than we had rest, and I had to fight our enemies on several different occasions. Safety would seem possible and we would spend sometimes up to three months in a village, but the enemy would just find out. I knew these were just holding places to regain strength; however it never seemed to be enough time before we needed to move again.

2. The Journey

We lived in this way until I was eighteen years of age and Irena was turning sixteen. Many things had changed over the years. Irena and I bickered over almost everything. I could never figure her out. I would have an idea, and she would have one of her own. We were down to eight horses and fifteen men, which included Emeth and Cadman, who was almost fifteen years of age and royal pain in my ass. There were only ten warriors out of the group, though they were all high of honor. We had been on the move, without rest, which made everyone irritable. We all needed a good night's rest for a change. Although times were tough, we were a family, however odd we were. The king had left me in charge long ago, but I was not a boy anymore; I was becoming a young man. I had proven myself worthy by fighting in battles and keeping the princess safe thus far. Our group was small, and everyone in it trusted each other with their lives, but ultimately we would all lay it down for Irena.

We had been traveling toward a nearby range to take shelter in any overhang or cave we may find and finally made our way to a rocky passage that lead deeper into the mountains.

"Great, more climbing," said Irena, looking dismayed. There was a valley nearby that could have a water source. Almost all the other directions hadn't turned out very good for us.

"Let's pass through, we know what lies behind us, we have to keep moving," I suggested. Everyone looked to me to make these sorts of decisions. As I was considering our options, we heard horses drawing near. We stopped and listened. I climbed some of the rocks to listen and to maybe get a look at who it was. The dark army was gaining on us. They had been trailing us for days, I knew, but I was surprised by their fast approach. I ran back down quietly and whispered, "We have to split up. There are at least twelve soldiers moving in this direction and will spot us shortly. Some of us need to lead them away from the princess; it's the only way."

"We can't split up now, our group is too small, it would be difficult to fight with only half our men." said Emeth.

"Alright, then, the army will assume the princess is with the largest group and continue to follow the horses' tracks. I will take Irena with me on foot in a different direction. We will still head north and meet you in a day's travel on the other side of these rocks." Emeth didn't much like the idea of me traveling alone with Irena. Our chances of being found by the relentless dark army were slimmer this way and agreed it was our best option. We couldn't risk Irena being captured.

I helped Irena off her horse, and we started to run. We had to make our way deeper into the rocks, so their horses would have a hard time getting through. The other men rode hard to get the army's attention, and like I expected, the army followed; the plan had worked. Irena and I continued moving for the rest of the day. I could tell she was exhausted. We found a cave and decided it was a good place to stay the night. Well, she decided of course. It was always her way; she frustrated me sometimes. I knew lighting a fire could be dangerous, someone might see the smoke and come investigate, but I lit a small one inside the cave so Irena could stay warm. The nights had grown cold.

I had begun expecting the worst anywhere we went. My eyes constantly searched and I kept the group always ready to move. Irena, however, was numb to this. She had hope in everything and thought it would all work out in the end. I wouldn't dare tell her I saw it as a lost cause. It seemed there was more evil in the world than there was good.

"Get some rest Irena; I'll be outside keeping watch."

I turned toward the cave entrance, "Wait, please don't go and leave me in here alone. I can't be left alone right now. You don't have to sleep outside, stay in here by the fire." It was an unusual request, but I sat back down. I could tell she was frightened. "Nothing had better happen to them because of me, I swear it."

"Everything will be fine," I assured her, though I doubted my own words.

"That didn't sound very convincing," she retorted.

After a minute or two she spoke again, "I am so sorry for always snapping at you, it's not very kind of me I realize, and I know you are only protecting me and have my best interest at heart. It's just that I don't want anyone else to sacrifice their life for me. I am ready to face him alone." It seemed she was telling me that all of her arguing over my direction was because she didn't want it to lead to me being hurt. It was a nice sentiment. She was a complete mystery to me.

"Irena, you know better than anyone that everything will be fine. Do not worry for me, or for anyone else. This is my destiny, remember? I am immortal after all," trying to comfort her. I nudged her and smiled; hoping to lighten her spirits and keep her from making that pitiful frown. She smiled sadly for a moment. She had always seemed so strong to me, even when her parents had died. I had never seen her this way before, and I didn't understand why it saddened me. I knew I had always protected her because it was what I was meant to do, but I realized it was only because I cared for her. I walked over to her. Her head was down, facing the ground, and she had tears falling. I sat beside her. "Irena please, don't cry." It killed me to see her this way. I held her chin gently before I knew what I was doing. I wanted her to look up at me; I wanted to see her face.

"You were right when you were a boy and you said you didn't ask for any of this. You shouldn't be spending your whole life protecting me; you should have a normal life."

"Irena, I may not have asked for this, but there's nowhere else I'd rather be." As I spoke and listened to my own words, I realized that this was how I truly felt. She looked up at me, amazed at my words as well. "We are fighting for a good cause, to keep you alive. After everything we've been through, we mustn't give up now," I added.

This was another moment for me that seemed frozen in time. I wish I could have frozen it forever. We sat for quite some time in silence, holding each other's gaze. She had beautiful eyes. It was as if she was looking straight into my soul and knew my heart completely.

"I wish we could be in my castle, going to one of my father's grand ceremonies for my sixteenth birthday or something special," she said. "We could have danced like we did when we were little." Her birthday was in one week.

Although it seemed silly, I asked her if that was what she really wanted. And then I asked her to dance with me, "Why not?" I said when she looked up at me in disbelief. We never had time for these sorts of things. We stood up without any music and I swayed her back and forth very slowly, holding her hands and turning her softly. She smiled and giggled as I twirled her, returning close to me before she laid her head on my shoulder.

"This is much easier for me now that I know what I'm doing." She laughed. The sound of her laughter was a treat for my ears. It was so nice enjoying each other's company, and I liked having her near me. She was warm and divine. Although we were on the run, she had a pleasant appearance and her hair looked as though she had just brushed it. I reached to touch it, and when she looked up at me I was struck by her beauty. I didn't know from where these feelings had come, but the thought was suddenly wonderful to me, so I leaned in and kissed her. Her taste was delicious. I drew back, realizing what I had done and wondering how she'd react. She was looking at me with a soft, warm smile. Although it was new, it seemed to have settled with both of us. She seemed to have enjoyed it as much as I had and with no signal of regret. I kissed her again holding her face in my hands. After a moment, I pulled away. "Goodnight," she said with a smile and went to lay down by the fire, still blushing, as I headed near the entrance of the cave. 'That was perfect,' I thought to myself. I imagined kissing her again as my eyes grew weary. Exhaustion took over, and I closed my eyes and drifted into a deep sleep. It was the best sleep I'd had in months, and I dreamt of Irena.

The next day we began to move again. There was a shift in the way we interacted. I asked her if she needed any help getting around the rocks and looked out for her even more carefully. We had grown up together, and I had forgotten our titles. And it suddenly dawned on me that she was royalty and should be treated as such. Either way she was a treasure to me. She was wearing a white gown and matching headpiece that had a jewel that hung down on her forehead. Her hair was as blonde as sunshine and her skin, fair. I held her carefully as we made our way over giant, jagged rock canopies. We came upon a stone bridge with dark green ivy up its sides that crossed over a stream and stopped to drink some of the water and sit in its shade. On the other side of the bridge was a forest, however, most of the trees were dead or hollow. It looked eerie and I decided I would rather wait for the others or head down the riverside than to take Irena into it. I had told the men we would meet them going north in a day's time, so we couldn't turn a different way. We didn't have much of an option. We could wait, but we weren't sure if we were ahead or they had already passed. After a few hours passed, we decided to walk a while, and if anything, we could turn back if we didn't find them. We started crossing the bridge, and I had a funny feeling we were being watched. I was searching the shadows in the dead forest when something emerging from behind a rock off the bridge caught my eye. It was two trolls making their way towards us. They were short, like dwarfs, and had large noses. They smelled of a foul odor and were hairy all over.

"Well, well, well, what do we have here?" said one of the trolls.

"Please, have you seen any horses come through here?"

"We don't help humans. This is our bridge, go back wherever you came from."

"We cannot, we must cross over this bridge and go into the forest," I demanded.

"No one crosses our bridge and no one dares go into the forest." I could tell the trolls weren't going to be of any help to us. Trolls rarely helped humans, but they did like to bargain and trade.

"Can we make a bargain with you and maybe give you something to let us pass?" said Irena.

"Well aren't you something pretty, what would you give us?" They were both laughing and teasing.

"Come on, Irena, they're not going to help us. I should make them let us pass," holding up my sword.

"No," Irena said, "what if I give you both one of my most valuable treasures?"

"What are we talking about, pretty, show us?" Irena took out her sea shell necklace that she had been keeping ever since we were children for good luck.

"Irena, don't! You don't have to give them that, we will find another way." She held up the necklace to show them and told them it was very valuable.

"I suppose we can make a deal just this time," said one of the trolls. I moved in front of Irena.

"I don't think this is a good deal. There must be another way; you shouldn't have to give them that."

Irena argued, "I don't see another option, unless you have another plan, we need to pass through."

If it were up to me I would've put up a fight with the trolls. Irena's gentle spirit, without my knowing, had only recently, tamed my wild nature and made me more considerate of her. Suddenly I was aware of my abrupt tendencies and noticed them. This time I would surrender my own will and let Irena have her way. I knew she would regret losing the necklace later when she had a moment to think on the loss. I promised myself to replace the lost necklace with something even more valuable someday. She handed it over. As we took our first steps into the gloomy forest, I began to wish we hadn't. It didn't feel right in it, with such a dramatic change in scenery with only a few steps. I didn't want to be in here long, I was only looking for a trace of horse hooves. We only had a couple of hours before sunset, and this wasn't the place to be caught after dark. If only I hadn't, in my sudden anger, pushed out the troll's banter of how no one returns once entering the dark forest.

3. The Forest

As we walked further into the forest I began to wish I hadn't disregarded the troll's words and actually listened to what they were muttering on about.

"Alright, there's no sign of anyone here," I said, "let's turn back." Irena was tired, and we had walked a couple of miles and still found no sign of tracks. It was very humid in the forest. We were only halfway back to the bridge when we stopped for a second to catch our breath. Irena was leaning against her nearest tree, when suddenly a claw reached up from under the ground and clasped her ankle. As I ran toward her, she screamed. The greenish hand with long, black fingernails pulled her to the ground and into a crevice of the gnarly tree stump. I looked into the space where she had disappeared and called for her, but there was no reply. I tried to dig, but the hole had shrunk up, consumed with sand again and there was nothing left. Panicking, I searched for a way under, but there was nothing. 'What was that thing?' I had to know. 'Those damn trolls would know.' I started running as fast as I could.

"TROLLS," I yelled! I screamed for them continuously until one popped up,

"You again; what do you want?"

"The girl I was with was pulled underground by a green hand. What was it? And how do I get her back?"

"Oh dear, the answer will cost you."

"I don't have time for your games; I have to save her now! Tell me!" I demanded.

"Give me your sword and I'll send you on your way."

"My sword?" I questioned. 'How was I supposed to defeat whatever that thing is without my sword?'

"That is my price for the answer," he said. I threw it over to him, my father's sword.

"Go down the river just a mile or so and you will see caves. Deep into the caves there will be tunnels, a goblin took her, probably planning to eat her for dinner if he hasn't already." 'A goblin, of course.' Goblins lived underground. I started running in the direction he pointed. "I warn you, boy, go down deep enough and you will end up straight in hell," he laughed and yelled to me as I ran toward my only hope of saving Irena.

The first cave I found I plunged into in a desperate hurry. There was no time to investigate the large space. It was too dark a place to see anyway, and squeezed in smaller and smaller the further I reached. I was eventually crawling. I felt around to continue deeper into the unknown darkness. This must be easier for trolls. I reached the end of the narrow tunnel, and it opened to another cavern. I crawled out, my eyes slowly adjusting, and I could hear water dripping from inside the caves. I moved in the direction I felt like she would have fallen and followed my instinct. I was unsure of what I could do without my sword. Hopefully I wouldn't be fighting a goblin with only my bare hands, which unfortunately was a good possibility. The thought occurred that I might even have to sacrifice myself to let Irena escape. I've heard that a goblin possesses various magical abilities and that they have very strong temperaments. I kept walking ahead which seemed like forever and still nothing. Deeper and deeper underground I went. Almost an hour had passed and I had traveled quickly through various tunnels. Suddenly, I heard a noise from around a corner. I crept quietly to see what it was. A goblin, I wasn't sure how many were down here or if it was even the same one that took her. I followed him for a while until I heard crying and moved towards the sound. He had passed from where the sound was coming from and kept walking further down the tunnel. There she was, balled up in a corner. Irena saw me and before she could make any kind of cry, I signaled her to be quiet. This must have been exactly where he pulled her under. There were large tree roots poking around the walls. Bones and skulls covered the ground all around. It was a dreadful place, and we were both full of fear. I quickly assessed Irena's ankle, which was scratched from where the goblin had grabbed her. I thought about what we should do. Would he catch up to us if we started running? Or would I need to catch him by surprise and jump him when he came back? I grabbed a large rock on the ground, and whispered to Irena, "let's go; follow me." Leaning around the corner to the way I saw him go, the tunnel was clear from what I could see. We quickly began down the tunnel from the direction I could remember. Running would echo, and we didn't need to make any noise, besides Irena was limping so we could not go fast. We made several turns and thought we were lost.

"You cannot run from me girl, I will find you!" he growled! His voice echoed through the tunnels and reached us. He noticed within minutes she was missing. He must not have been far behind. We started running.

"This way," I said and we started down another tunnel. I was sure this was the right way out. Irena was breathing heavily and limping because of her leg. "Come on!" I said, almost there. We turned the next corner, almost to the end and there he was, standing right in front of my face. He was tall and green with long, pointy ears and sharp nails.

"Stand back, goblin!" I yelled. He stepped back not having expected me, and then his eyes shifted as if noticing I was without a weapon.

"I knew I smelt another," he licked his lips.

"We are leaving," I said angrily.

"Really, how do you think?" he sneered with a crooked smile. "I don't see any weapon on you." I took the stone and gashed him with it aside the head. He turned and bit me in the arm. It was the most pain I had ever felt. Irena let out a scream, and as soon as he was on top of me Irena lifted her hands and a great bright light shot out of her at the goblin. It shot him across the other side of the tunnel and I got up and we started to run out. "In here," I pushed Irena through the hole that we needed to crawl out of. We got to where we could stand and started running towards the light poking through the end of the cave. We could see it. Light, the feeling was incredible, hope that we might make it out. The goblin came through the hole and was right behind us. We finally reached the light and ran out. The goblin did not follow us out because of the bright light shining from outside; he wasn't used to it. Whatever Irena did in there had burned him. He couldn't be in the light. He was made for darkness.

"I curse you," he yelled from inside the cave. "Do you hear me? *I CURSE YOU!*"

Curse, I thought, like we weren't already living in one. It had only just become sunrise outside. Thank goodness for morning light or the goblin could have followed us out from the cave. My arm hurt very badly. I grabbed Irena and held her close.

"Are you alright?" I asked Irena.

"I'm fine. My ankle hurts a little, how did you find me? I thought I was lost down there and would never see you again." She explained.

"I am destined to always find you, remember?" I had never been so scared for her in my life. It was a complete miracle that I found her down there and that we made it back out safely. We were both so happy to see each other and some light again from outside. The darkness was dreadful. I guessed more than a night down there would make a man go insane.

"What happened down there Irena? What was that you did?"

"I don't know? That's never happened before. Whatever it was happened because I saw you in danger," she said.

"You saved me this time."

"We saved each other," she replied.

"No more eerie forest from this point forward. Now let me look at your ankle." It looked bad. Those hideous nails tore and ruined her beautiful skin and she was still bleeding.

"I'm fine; let me look at your arm."

This was not good, the bite had only just happened and it was already turning a greenish purple color, slowly through my veins. This had to be poisonous from what I could tell. The color traveled up through my arm within the next few minutes. We needed to find somewhere someone would know about these bites and scratches that could help us and tell me what I could do for them. At this point I didn't have a clue what direction to take. We were still in the woods and moved alongside the river, till eventually we found green trees that looked like a normal forest again. We continued to walk the entire afternoon without any sign of anyone else nearby. We were in this forest alone. By this time I could barely walk. The poison was making me sick. Irena was limping and started to run a fever. It seemed she had an infection from the scratches. I was getting dizzy and my vision was becoming blurred. There was no one around us for miles and still no sign of the others from our group. We both knew we couldn't make it much longer. We needed some help fast.

"Sit here for a moment and I will keep walking and find someone to help," she said.

"NO, Irena not by yourself."

"You can't keep going on like this; I will be back before nightfall." I couldn't argue with her. I was too weak.

I had no other answer, "Please be careful," I let out with a very small breath. She kissed my forehead, tore off a piece from her dress and wrapped my wound, and then started walking. I watched her disappear into the thick green forest.

Irena walked on for hours and became nauseous from the infection. She was very ill, but kept going and fighting through the sickness. She was worried about Alick. She knew she had to find help quickly or he may die. Her leg hurt very badly, but she endured it and kept limping forward because it was all she could do. She stopped by a stream and washed the scratches with some water. It made her cuts a little more bearable if only for a moment. Since it made no difference to the way she was feeling she knew Alick could only be getting worse too. She was extremely worried about him. If she were to die, it would be the end of Avalon.

Her fever grew higher and she had an aching headache and it became hard to think. It was only about an hour before sunset and still nothing in sight. She promised she would be back before nightfall and knew he would only try and look for her if she wasn't back by then, but she had to keep going. If she was to return empty handed she knew what the outcome would be and that wasn't an option. She became very dizzy and tripped and fell down on the ground into the leaves and moss around her. The forest was thick and the tree stumps were large and round. She started breathing softly and felt faint. She knew she couldn't give up after everything Alick had done for her. Her vision was getting blurry now. She could not move or stand. Her body was stiff and she had no energy left to push her body back up. She could not think straight because of the fever and throbbing headache. Irena passed out into the deep enchanted forest as sunset grew closer to a near.

Alick had been sitting against a tree and in and out of consciousness the entire time. He was hallucinating. He thought he kept seeing Irena in the distance and then she would disappear. He called for her, but no reply. He felt sick to his stomach and vomited. His arm looked ten times worse than before. You could see exactly where each tooth went into the flesh. It was bleeding and puss drained out from the infection. He could no longer feel his arm anymore. He would pass out for a few minutes then force himself to open his eyes. He thought Irena should be back by now. He tried to stand but could not. He was extremely dehydrated and felt as if he were about to die. He needed Irena to be back. If he were to die he needed to tell her he loved her. He needed her to know he would come back and find her in another life. Even if he doubted what everyone said about him, he needed to believe it were true now. He had so many things he wished to say to her before he would die and he did not want to die here alone without her. He closed his eyes and drifted off once more.

Irena was still lying on the ground when she woke up and looked around. Everything was still hazy to her. She heard a noise, something walking in the leaves near her direction. She looked over and could not believe her eyes. Standing there in front of her was a white unicorn. She had only heard of this rare wild creature from ancient stories. Very few people rarely got to see one. It was walking towards her, but she was not frightened. She sat up and grabbed its nose. It had a large pointed horn on its forehead. As she touched it she immediately felt better. Her fever had gone down and her scratches disappeared before her eyes. She never knew if the stories were all true. It was said that a unicorn's horn had healing powers. She rubbed the soft unicorn for a while to see if it would stay calm enough for her to climb on its back. The unicorn knelt down and she climbed upon its back, grabbed its mane, and headed back to Alick in a hurry. She finally had hope that things would be alright now. It was getting dark. When she got there she jumped down and hurried over to him.

"Alick", she was crying for him. "Please come back to me, Please!" She kissed his lips and held him tightly.

"Irena," my voice was low. "Thank goodness you're alright, I was beginning to worry." She could tell it was hard for me to get out my own words. I was muttering something that felt like the right words, but I could tell she could not understand what I was trying to say. I looked up and saw the beautiful creature standing before me.

"Your leg is better," I saw.

"Yes, try to stand, I will help you. You must touch the unicorn so it can heal your wound." I could barely move and leaned against the nearest tree, but I could not stand on my own. Irena brought the unicorn over to me. I rubbed the unicorns' neck. As I looked at my arm, the green in my veins vanished slowly as if it was never there. Amazing I thought, I can't believe it. Instantly the pain was gone. Of course Irena would be able to find and capture a creature so pure. It was said that only a virgin could capture a unicorn. The unicorn was a symbol of purity and grace. Irena standing beside the enchanting creature with her white gown proved all the stories were true. Irena's name meant peace, she represented life itself. She was pure hearted and good. They looked as if they both belonged together. Not only were we both healed, but felt as though we had more energy than we had ever had before. When Alick helped Irena up on top of the beautiful creature there was another spark between them like the one they had felt before when they were just children.

"Why do you think that happens sometimes when we touch?" I asked.

"I'm not sure exactly, but I think it has something to do with our energy together. If we are destined to find each other by fate, then maybe it has something to do with us being meant for one another as well." She replied.

"You really believe that," I asked curious for her answer.

"Of course," she replied.

"Irena, I thought I was going to die and you were the only thing that kept going through my mind. I wanted you to be with me so I could tell you how I felt before it was too late. I love you Irena. I love you more than I can put into words," I said, not knowing how she would respond. Then she kissed me. This was a much longer kiss than before and full of passion. It felt so right holding her in my arms; I never wanted to let her go. We were young and full of life and now full of love. Pure love is the only thing that kept us going day by day from that moment on. We had almost lost each other once; we weren't taking any more chances with anything. Any decisions I would make from that moment on that risked putting her in any sort of danger, would be skipped. Even if it somehow benefited us in some great way, it still wasn't worth the risk to me. We did get caught in a few situations where we had no other choice but to go across them. Like a swamp we came across, I led the unicorn through and told Irena to stay put on its back. I knew this place was dangerous. I could tell the unicorn could sense what direction the danger was coming from so I walked where the unicorn lead. Without this creature's instinct we wouldn't have made it through certain places. We came upon a pond with fresh water one day and decided it was a good place to drink and bathe. I swung in on a vine into the water and from a distance. I watched Irena behind a glare of sunshine take off her dress and dive in with only her under garments. She swam over and stopped about five feet in front of me. We sat there staring at each other for a long time, never touching. I knew if I did I wouldn't be able to stop myself, although I wanted to stay in that pool with her forever just so I could keep looking at her. Those few days we were lost in one another. She teased me so. I don't think she intended to, although she enjoyed herself.

Irena's beauty could only be compared to an angel. That was the best way I could describe her glow. We camped under a tree that night gazing up at the stars, then walked for a few more days with the unicorn until we reached the end of the enchanted forest and it was time to set the wild creature free. It was meant to be free like Irena. She thanked the unicorn for all of its help and released it into the wild. We watched the beautiful creature disappear back into the forest and then continued to walk until we reached grit that soon became a large desert. Looking out ahead of us was continuous sand dunes farther than the eye could see. There was seldom a cactus visible. I estimated we were somewhere close to the country Indias. We went through many strange villages made out of clay and we eventually found Emeth, Cadman, and a few men that lasted from out of our small group. Some didn't make it, but we were relieved that the others did and that we were all together again. Although we were down to only two soldiers left to help protect us, Irena was ecstatic we had gained back our family. Emeth was like a father to her.

The princess started dressing without any jewels or pearls and into normal gowns that would not stick out, but no matter what she wore Irena's beauty was noticed. It was safer this way. We had learned to be more discreet. Emeth explained that the rest of the group led the dark army off and then they got separated and lost. They had been looking for us ever since, not knowing if the other men were dead or still alive. "At least we found each other," I said. We told them our story of the goblin and how a unicorn saved us in the end. Emeth caught on quickly to the changes of Irena and my feelings for one another. They grew stronger every day. We forgot our titles; any other life I would not belong with her. Irena was like a forbidden fruit only worthy of a king or prince. I was intrigued by her beauty and the mystery about her. Anywhere we traveled Irena's beauty was admired by everyone who had saw her. Anyone who met her loved her. I couldn't blame them, and I had fallen completely and madly in love with her for myself. Often her beauty was not a positive trait for us; we found ourselves in several fights over it with the wrong sorts of men because they had come too close to her. I knew for the time being we must keep her hidden if at all possible. When we went through small towns she kept quiet with her head down and face covered. Every day she showed me beauty in everything and taught me that life was a gift. We could tell her power was growing stronger. She was still unsure of how to use it.

4. Distractions

We walked for weeks in the hot desert sun. The sand dunes kept on going and never seemed to end. The desert was hot and dry with almost unbearable temperatures. We saw nothing for days. Even though we were short on water; it was nice not having to worry about running into anyone or having anything around us for a while. Whenever we were around others we had some sort of trouble. I grew tired of seeing people. The desert was uncomfortable, but safe and while others wouldn't ever consider it a break, we could finally relax and be ourselves without worries, except for water. I was very grateful we found the others, but I also missed the time alone with Irena, which we seldom had so very little of now. The days were hot and miserable and the nights grew cold. One night I saw Irena shaking in her sleep because she was freezing so I went over to lie down beside her to keep her warm. Emeth never questioned what was going on between us. He figured it out and knew we were the only two people that were immortal so it was understandable how we became so close having that in common, we needed each other and no one else could relate. He understood how, with the given circumstances, we could fall in love with each other so easily. I thought it would be a problem when people started finding out our feelings for each other, but it was almost as if everyone expected it to happen eventually. We walked for weeks until we finally figured out we could no longer go on like this and we started questioning what we should do differently. Water was seldom found and food was scarce in the desert. Not to mention the heat was rising the further south we traveled. After a few more days and miles to the south, we came upon a city. The city was almost as large as Avalon from what I could remember. The walls that protected it were even larger. This great city was in the middle of the desert. Travelers were moving east and west of the city on camels and elephants, which explained why we never ran into any one else from the direction we were traveling. We were dying of thirst and the city was mesmerizing. I almost questioned aloud if it were real. We were all drawn to it. Inside, we spoke with a few people and heard about the great queen that ruled here. We never met anyone who didn't dislike Damion besides his army. And after we felt safe enough from what we saw inside the castle walls, we announced ourselves to Queen Sahara. She had been brought up from Egypt and moved here to marry the king who died a year after. The Egyptian queen was young and had jet black hair and a sun kissed body that was dressed very much revealing. She wore a sheath black gown that was showing through and gold Egyptian jewelry with a matching gold head piece. I thought it was very unusual that she also had a black panther as a pet sitting by her side at her throne on a gold chained leash. She was intrigued with our story of how we escaped Damion and his dark army and how we ended up here. She had heard of Princess Irena and of her immortality. Most great rulers had, even when royals usually kept it a secret from peasants. Royals had advisors and spies to bring them all their important information. The way she was obsessed with Irena made me question her motives. Like others who had learned of Irena, I watched her reactions very closely. Emeth spoke with her and told her of our long tiresome journey and asked her if we could stay for a few days to rest. She decided to help protect us here inside her walls. The queen offered us safety and told us we could stay as long as we wished. She treated us as her royal guests. We had fresh clothes and plenty of food. Irena loved it here; it reminded her of her home in Avalon. Irena tried out the queens' Egyptian styled dresses made from the royal couturiers that were bright and colorful. I wasn't a fan of the styles or choices, but had to admit anything she wore looked gorgeous on her. There were parties and dances every night at dinner. The food was like nothing I had ever tasted before, full of spices and herbs. My favorite dish was of hummus. The queen replaced my lost sword with a small dagger. Irena followed the queen everywhere and copied anything she did. The world had been hung at our feet and still something about it here didn't seem quite right to me. The others were convinced we should stay for a while. I reminded Irena that we could not stay here long and needed to start moving again in the next couple of days.

"You shouldn't get too comfortable, a week at the most," I told her.

"It's safe here, you shouldn't need to worry anymore," she would tell me back.

"Irena everyone wants what you have, remember there will always be someone with the wrong motives after it. Nowhere is completely safe for someone like you."

"These walls have never been breached. Damion doesn't know we are here, and the queen has promised to keep us protected and hidden. Look at all she has done for us." She argued. "Be grateful and enjoy it. We can finally have a normal life here. We don't have to keep running. The queen has given me her word. She is our friend."

I knew this was going to be hard to convince her otherwise and long arguments continued over the next few hours. I guessed when it came down to it, I would probably have to throw Irena over my shoulder and drag her out of here myself.

"I gave my father my word and promised to protect you and I promise you now we are leaving in a couple of days so enjoy this and soak it all in while you can!"

Irena huffed, "we shall see about that!" And she stomped off to join the party.

As I sat down to eat supper I watched her dancing and laughing. The dancing here was exotic; not like from home. I then caught out of the corner of my eye queen Sahara staring at me from across the room as if she knew I wanted to leave. Every time I saw the queen she was almost half naked. I did not like the intense look she was giving me. It made me want to leave even more. I promised myself that night that I would give Irena the time she deserved to get the fun she needed to have out of her system. I did admit to myself she needed this after all we had been through, but we had rules and routine that we always stuck to no matter what. And we would be leaving whether she hated me for it or not. We needed to keep moving. Sooner or later word would spread we were here. I would give her a couple more days to be treated like the princess she always was. I left her alone that night to do as she wished. I decided I would bring up the topic again in the morning when we both had the chance to calm down. I had heated things up with her several times so I gave her some space, not that she even noticed. She was always by the queens' side.

Finally the next afternoon I found her sitting alone in the garden area. There were pillars holding the walls up around the open ceiling in the middle, half indoors and outdoors and enough plants to get lost inside the small room and a bathing pond with waterfalls overflowing the gardens. She was sitting with her feet in the pool of water when I found her. The maids who were fanning her left her side when they saw me enter.

"I'm sorry I have been keeping to myself and so distant, but I love it here, I don't want to leave, the queen is my friend. She told me we could stay," Irena apologized.

"Irena I know this is the first time you have been treated like royalty. And you should have always been treated this way before, I get it, but something about this place is unsettling to me."

"What are you saying? We have been treated with nothing but kindness."

"I know it seems that way and I can't explain it, but my gut instinct is telling me we should go soon. Everything seems too good to be true."

"Please wait a few more days; I'm just not ready yet." I couldn't help but agree with her from the pouting face she was giving and then she playfully splashed me with the pool water and then I pushed us both in. We were laughing and kissing. I had missed her the past week. I pushed her up against the wall. She looked as though she desperately wanted me to kiss her again. So I did. This kiss was unlike all the other times before, this time faster and more aggressive. Neither one of us wanted to stop.

"We must get out of here and get you a dry gown."

"What if I don't want to?" she grinned teasingly.

"Don't tempt me Irena; we must get out of here before we do something foolish." I held her hand and helped her out of the water. She looked down at me, standing there in front of me in her soaked tight dress. She leaned in once more and gently kissed my lips, "as you wish," and her fingertips left my hand slowly as she turned and walked away. I almost grabbed her hand and pulled her back to me, but I knew if I kissed her that way again I wouldn't be able to control myself. Irena was not ready for me or anyone in that sort of way and I had plans to marry her first, if she would have me. I eagerly yearned for her. Every kiss with her was better than the kiss before; a spectacular experience. I had noticed Irena was acting differently and not like her usual self; all the more reason for us to leave. But we were so caught up in that moment together that we didn't even notice that queen Sahara was standing on top of her balcony, carefully watching us from up above the entire time.

Late that night, after dinner time, I was given a message that the queen requested to speak with me of something of great importance and it could not wait. I could not turn down her request while we were staying as her guest and after all the generosity she had shown to us. So I went up to her chamber that night unsure of what this meeting could be about. As I entered the room the light was dim. Fire torches were on every surrounding wall. Her black panther's eyes stuck out from the darkness across the room. She was spread out on a long bench staring at me as I walked in. Like always, she barely had any material covering her body, this time, a little less.

"Come in," She was also petting a large snake wrapped around her with very particular markings. If I had to guess, it looked poisonous with such unique markings.

"You have a very interesting pet choice," I said, trying to lighten the mood. She didn't reply. "You wish to speak to me of something now at this late hour?" I questioned her further, eagerly waiting for an answer.

"Yes, it couldn't wait any longer." She replied. "Please shut the door behind you." I hadn't the slightest idea what this was all about. I closed it slowly and watched her carefully; I could not read her. Maybe this was why I felt so uncomfortable around her. She was in her own way beautiful and the complete opposite of Irena. Something about her was intoxicating. There was also something very sad about her eyes, but like the city you could get drawn to her as well. Irena had been drawn to her the entire stay and did not want to leave her side. I admitted to myself that I sort of liked the ways I felt when I was around her also, so I instantly knew my being here was wrong, and that I should leave immediately.

I questioned her again, "What is this all about?" Still unsure of why I was here.

"This is about you Alick. Why you are unhappy with your stay here? Haven't I provided you with everything you need? Something seems to be missing for you. Why would you want to leave my palace and take Irena on a never ending journey? To where exactly? This place is the safest place you have both ever been and exactly what you both need and want, wouldn't you agree?"

"Yes, but we told you when we came it was only temporary until we gained our strength back. I'm sure you must understand that we need to keep moving. Nowhere is completely safe for someone like Irena, and I must always protect her. We thank you for treating us as your guest, but we must leave first thing in the morning. Surely you can understand."

"You do more than protect her don't you? Maybe you're letting your love for her cloud your judgment and not seeing clearly that this is where she wants to be. She belongs with royalty." The queen was toying with my mind and my emotions, and for a minute, it was working until I had a thought that this was how she had been convincing Irena into staying. Irena had not been herself since we had arrived here. Queen Sahara walked slowly towards me in a very seductive way. Her black lace gown, if you could call it a gown, was showing off her skin, the slits were up to her thigh, and dragging the floor behind her. Her garments left little to the imagination. She was an irresistible woman.

She was very close now and began to speak to me again in almost a whisper, "Irena needs to marry a king or prince, someone who can truly protect her with an army, you don't have any chance with her, and she has already chosen this place over you. She won't ever leave now. She is young and naïve. She will grow older and realize she can have anyone she wants and do better than you. I can tell by the look on your face that you know it's true and that you have your own desires as well." She slid her hand down my chest and I suddenly guided her off. She turned my head back as I turned away. "I can fulfill those desires if you stay." The temptation was rising, trying to resist the favor and not give into this urge. I wanted no other woman except for Irena. The queen was why Irena had been acting so strange. There was no telling what thoughts the queen tricked her into thinking. The queen was vindictive and manipulating. Irena was in my head and I could not think of anything else but her. Irena was who I craved.

"Irena has my heart I cannot accept your offer," I said. Any other man would not have been able to resist. It was not disappointment or understanding in the queens eyes. What was it? It was something else. I searched for the right words in my head. Was it anger, fury, or revenge?

"No one can resist me. I will not be rejected!" She stormed toward the doorway about to exit into another room and then turned to me the last time, "What a waste, so young and handsome. Why don't you stay and get to know my panther a little while longer. Luna is very hungry, and she hasn't had anyone to eat in about three days. Poor thing's starved."

She slammed the door behind her and, as I started for the door, I watched the demon cats eyes glow in the dark watching back at me. Locked! All the doors were locked. The large black panther showed itself from out of the corner. I held out my dagger. We circled the room facing one another. The large cat looked as if it was going to pounce any second. I threw vases and whatever I could grab to distract it while I thought, but I knew that wouldn't work, and it only made the animal angrier. It growled and tried to grab me with its large claws. I stayed out in the open so I would not get caught in a corner with the panther. Finally, it came forward and I knew it would try and wrap its claws around me as it bit through my neck. I swung my knife as it got closer and scratched its face as it jumped at me once again infuriated. With one hand I pushed the face and with the other I stuck the knife deep into the heart of the beast; as hard as I could. The animal fell on top of me and landed deep onto the dagger with so much force we both fell to the ground. I was not hurt only crushed by the heavy cat. After some struggle I finally became free from the dead animal above me. I was knocked out of breath briefly from the heavy fall, checking the rest of myself for marks, but the cat's claws had only scratched my armory. What a relief. I then kicked through one of the locked doors. I had to find Irena and we had to get out of the city tonight.

5. The Escape

Irena was supposed to be in her chamber at night, but was out in the garden looking up at the stars. Confused at all the queen had told her since she had spent her time there. She loved the way she had felt and maybe the queen was right - Alick might not be meant for her. But she thought about all that had happen between them earlier that day, which was a reminder of how they were together, and all they had been through and how they had grown together. The feelings reassured her that Alick was right, and they needed to leave. She knew the queen was wrong, and she loved Alick with all her heart and, in the morning, she would tell him exactly how she felt. She wanted him, all of him for forever and always, as long as she was alive. She was sure, even if that meant running, never being in one place long enough, having nothing, never secure. At least they would still have each other and that was all she ever truly needed. She turned to head back to her chambers and, to her surprise; Queen Sahara was standing right behind her.

"Oh, you scared me, what is wrong?" she asked.

"Save it! Shut up; Perfect Princess Irena that everyone wants to die for, I will give everyone their wish! You are so pretty and full of life. Would you like to know what I do to life? I take it!" She pulled Irena to her, grabbing her by the throat, and started sucking the breath out of her.

"STOP," I yelled! "Leave her alone!" Irena fell to the floor drained and coughing.

"How did you…" she paused. "Where is Luna? My panther better be alive or I will break my promise to Damion and kill her right now."

"You are helping Damion? I knew it."

"Not soon enough I'm afraid, and, yes, he promised to spare my city if I turned her over to him. I promised him he could have her alive, but it's so tempting not to take her beautiful soul all for myself. Do you know how many years I would stay young and live for if I sucked the beauty out of her right now? What a shame. I would have taken your life, too, if I could have gotten close enough to you. Now I'm afraid I must leave you two to the dark army." I saw flames flickering down the halls and heard the marches of heavy steps coming for us. In a hurry I grabbed Irena's hand and lead her fast down the hallways. Then I saw more lights coming from the opposite way. The soldiers were everywhere now. How could we escape the city? I pushed Irena inside the first door I could get to open.

"This is my fault; I should have listened to you! We should have left when you said. I'm sorry." Irena was crying profusely as we were running.

"No Irena, the queen tricked you, this isn't your fault. Come, we must get out of here quickly before they find us." The city was a maze. We could quickly become lost in it and captured if we took a wrong turn. We came up on a passageway that lead straight into Irena's chambers. I peaked in and no harm was in sight so I shut the door quickly behind us and barricaded the door with every heavy item I could find in the room. The window was not far from the ground outside - only about twenty feet or so. I could drop Irena down and jump behind her. Emeth would be getting the horses ready by now after he saw the dark army enter the city. We were always prepared for this just in case they came. He was always on the lookout and had a backup plan if it came to this.

"Irena, listen to me, we don't have much time. I have so many things I must tell you before you go."

"What? You're coming too!" I said nothing. She paused and started to panic when I didn't respond. "Alick, you can't leave me. I can't do this alone! I'll stay and fight with you; I will not leave without you."

"Irena you are not strong enough yet. You are still unsure of how your powers actually work, and we both know that you're not ready to face Damion, so I won't let you. I know it's not the time and you do, too. You're our only chance, you must leave now. This is the only way you have a chance of escaping. I must stay here to fight and hold them off while you get out of the city."

"NO, there has to be another way!"

"There isn't Irena, and there's no time to discuss it any further. I must do this and you must get out now before the city is swarmed with more soldiers from the dark army. Our lives are linked. I will find you in another life. We will be together again I promise." Tears fell and she grabbed my hand and put her face to mine.

"I love you Alick, I will always wait for you my darling. I promise."

"And I will always look for you until I find you my love. Promise me you'll stay near the oceans. Any other life I'm sure I will always love the sea as much as I do now and try to be near it." She wrapped herself around me not wanting to let go.

"Fate will bring us together again," she reminded me. "I will always look for you." The door started pounding.

"Search everywhere," a guard shouted! Suddenly, standing down in front of the window waiting with the horses, there was Emeth and Cadman waiting below.

"Stay invisible, it will be harder for Damion to find you if you stay out of large cities and keep to yourself. Try not to be noticed." She kissed me, my last kiss, and bittersweet.

"I'm so sorry for not listening to you," she apologized again.

"Irena stop, you are not to blame. Now GO!" This was it; Time to face him finally - the man who killed my father. I've fantasized how this moment would be ever since we left Avalon. She whispered in my ear "*I love you*," as I dropped her down with a light fall and watched from the window as my heaven vanished into the night with only two soldiers left to protect her. This was truly a tragic love story, never being together for enough time before having to run or get separated. Our romance was filled with sadness. Hopefully my father was right about my mark and I would be born again after death. I took down an old antique sword from the wall. It was rusty and unsharpened, which meant I had to swing even harder to break through skin. All that mattered to me now was that Irena had escaped, which gave me the only hope I had left to hold onto. She was my hope for the future. I turned to take my place and face the darkness waiting for me on the other side of the door. The banging continued as I waited. The soldiers finally busted through the doors. They were quick and fierce. One after another I struck them down. I yelled as I attacked the next ones to enter; I knew I had to kill as many as possible so that there would be less of a chance for more soldiers to follow Irena later. There were dozens lying on the floor around me when he approached the doorway. Finally, the moment I had been imagining for so long. He had dark black, greyish hair. His eyes were dark; looking straight into them felt like looking into a grave.

"So you are the one I have been hearing of; giving my men such a hard time." His voice was deep and low.

"I've been giving *you* trouble?" I sighed sarcastically.

"We meet at last," He said.

"You killed my father."

He looked around at all of his dead soldiers lying on the ground. Ignoring my statement, "You did all this yourself? Very brave, no one has ever taken on this many of my soldiers before and lived."

"This isn't the first of your soldiers I've fought, and I have killed many more. I've been running from you ever since you took over Avalon. I'm ready to stand and fight and avenge my father. The princess is safe, she has escaped once more and you will never find her!" He was furious with my words; I could tell no one had ever spoken to him in this way before. "I'm not frightened of you!" I added when he said nothing in return.

"Well you should be. Yes, I've been trying to find the princess for, like you've said, seven years now, and I'm tired of this chase. You have been a great part in causing her to escape further away from me. Once I kill you I will find her."

I went towards him and swung the bloody sword with both hands. He met my swing with his own sword and we continued to fight with our swords for several minutes or so. He had me against a wall pressing his sword close to my neck. I used my dagger to slice the only part I could reach with the only strength I had left. I cut his leg very deep. And he pierced the side of my hip as he let off my neck from the cut. I fell for a second, blood dripping from my side. I got back on my feet and raised my sword once more. We were both wounded and he knew I would stay relentless. Any other fight to death between two men would have been fought fairly, but he wasn't the type to lose. He would not fight fair, so he used his dark powers on me. I heard Irena screaming and the darkness swallowed me into its nightmare. I was blinded by the black dream for a moment when I felt his power strike me once more as a lightning bolt. I cried out in agony. The pain shot through me all over. The pain was so horrible that I wanted to die. "Irena," I whispered with light breath as I lay there watching my blood spread all over the floor around me. It was almost over. I would find her I told myself, I must remember, I must. I let out my last breath and looked death straight in the face and it kissed me. Everything went black and quickly faded away. The pain was gone.

PART 2

6. A New Beginning

Free at last! This new feeling I had been holding onto for so long, which seemed forever and a day overdue. I had finally become twenty two years of age and able to do anything I'd choose. I traveled here to be near the sea only recently. I was raised by a farmer who recently died; becoming ill in old age. I had never met my parents; I'm told they left me as a baby. I grew up on a farm and worked hard to pay my endless debt to the farmer that took me in, who didn't leave me defenseless to die alone and hungry. Something about my life was always missing. I traveled very far to see this city by the sea. It had been my dream for so long and now I finally had arrived. Avalon had always called out my name. Traveling to see the city for myself was the only thing I had ever dreamt of as long as I could remember. The city was abandoned and in ruins. Vines grew up all of the sides of what was left. I had a strange feeling of déjà vu' as I walked under the front gates leading into the city. I walked down the deserted roads as if I had been here sometime before. There were only a few people who lived outside of the city in a small village nearby. People stared at me suspiciously as I passed through the roads leading towards the city. No one had been here recently from what I could tell. Almost every building was abandoned. The people who were here obviously liked to keep to themselves. I had plans to travel to many other places in the world, but I wanted to start with Avalon first since it intrigued me so much with all of its history. I kept walking through all of the paths which seemed oddly familiar, as if my feet knew exactly where they were taking me. I eventually stepped up to the tallest tower and looked out over the city and the view of the ocean. The sun shining on the water was glorious. The top of the water sparkled and was almost blinding with its' reflection. Looking at the view was outstanding with the ocean reaching as far as the eye could see, looking as though it was never-ending. How I wanted to be sailing on the water. Sailing was a vision I had of myself that I had always eagerly thought would someday come true. I had never been this close to the sea before, I only dreamt of the sea from stories and tales I had heard when growing up. Could this be real? My imagination never came so close to comparing with reality. Finally I was here ready to start my own new adventure and start a life of my own. The life I had always wanted for myself could finally start today and nothing was holding me back.

I had a vague flashback of an imagined conversation I had with someone here, in exactly the same place where I was standing. Everyone always told me I had too large of an imagination. Even though this sort of thing happened to me often, this time it was different, it seemed more real. Everything about this place seemed like a life I had already lived. These feelings that overcame me didn't make any sense. I had never been here before. But this place seemed more real to me than the life I'd been living for the past twenty two years. How do I explain it? It felt as though I had been here before in my dreams. Something here called out my name and I couldn't figure it out why. My plan when I first arrived here was to stay a few days, look around, and move on to see another destination on my list. Now I thought maybe I should stay a little while longer. It felt like home to me, maybe I could make this my new home. I had no family missing me except Dara. She was a girl I had known for many years, always chasing me around when we were younger and interested in whatever I was doing. She had brown hair and green eyes. Before I left she begged me not to go, but she had always known that I wasn't going to stick around. I had plans to see the world. I could never become interested in her for some reason. Sure we would have been great together; we were the same age and looked a lot alike. People always said we were perfect for one another, but one evening we kissed and there wasn't anything there, no spark. In my head I always imagined a spark with a first kiss. And when it wasn't like I had expected, I told her some long story about how I didn't feel ready for this and how I thought we should just stay friends. Her parents thought someday we would marry until I left the small town and never promised if I would return or not. I suppose I could have brought her along with me. Although I could never get into the relationship, I knew I would never be able to stay content; something was just never there for Dara and me.

That night I dreamed of her again; the girl I had only seen in my dreams. She was young, standing on the shore of a beach, sunlight in her hair; the waves swishing back and forth breaking through the rocks. I had the same dream for as long as I could remember. Something about that night sleeping in the city of Avalon made the dream more real than ever before. I felt as though I could almost reach out and touch the girl standing there staring back at me. "Alick," the girl called out my name. I awoke and looked up at the stars. The dream felt so real that I was disappointed to awake from it. It was hard to sleep much that night from the excitement. Not only was I happy to be able to start a new life for myself, but also I was hoping I would find something here that I was longing for. My heart felt as though it had a large gaping hole that needed to be filled. I wanted to find whatever was missing and being here did not instantly give me the comfort or satisfaction I was looking for. When morning came I walked to the nearby village to ask questions about what had happened here years ago at Avalon. I studied the history and this place was destroyed not too long ago and everything about it intrigued me so dearly. There were stories and legends I had heard of a beautiful immortal princess that escaped from here and of the warrior boy who helped her and in the end lay down his life for hers. I heard these stories a hundred times back from where I was from, only it was much more interesting being heard by people that were originally from here and occasionally someone who experienced those days first hand. Whenever I did find someone that could personally remember those days for themselves, the memories they had mesmerized me, and interested me even more. Everyone in the world feared Damion ever since I was a child. The boy who wounded him killed him. He had lived only months after and died from the infection of his wounded leg, but not before having a son with an evil queen named Sahara. Before he died, he let out all of his dark powers upon the pregnant queen. His son was now around my age and carried on his father's wishes to capture the princess and destroy her along with anyone standing in the way. Only he didn't want everlasting life for himself like his father before him. He wanted to live forever to torture and punish the princess because he blamed her for his father's death. Revenge was all he cared about. I heard he was harsher than his father before him, except, from the stories people had told of Damion, I couldn't imagine how it could ever be possible for someone to be so cruel. From all of the tales I had overheard, I believed there was some truth to the stories. The other folk stories were just rumored and written down for the imagination; however, the people that I had met here seemed to believe them all true.

"You're in for a treat lad," a man said to me. "The princess's army passes by on ships every three years in honor of her father King Theron, her mother the Queen Isadora, and her long lost love. It should only be a few more days from now before they pass by here."

"Hush you," a woman poked at him. "No one speaks of these topics to strangers."

"Ah ma, he's only a young lad by himself interested in story tales, no harm done."

"No one ever comes around here asking questions and nosing around, go on now lad off with you before you be getting yourself into some trouble," the woman replied.

I never intended to cause any harm by staying here, so I picked up my belongings and left them standing there, shaking their heads and watching me go. If the tales were true, and the princess was still alive she would be around almost forty years of age and I had to see for myself. I doubted she had any magic; however I decided to stay a few more days in case I could manage to see the ships pass by and, hopefully, maybe even the princess waving. The thought never crossed my mind to believe in immortality. There was no way the princess could still be alive in her twenties. Once I had seen for myself, it would prove there was no such thing as immortality and the stories could only be false. Convincing myself, I could then leave and be happy and travel to any other place. Then I decided I could leave this place content with my decision and move on to another. I kept to myself and stayed away from the village so I wouldn't cause any unnecessary problems. People here liked to keep to themselves and obviously didn't like anyone snooping around, especially me with my questions.

The next morning the commotion and noise suddenly awoke me. I could hear people waving and cheering. In the distance I could see ships coming our way. I couldn't help but have a huge grin on my face. Filled with excitement, I ran down to get a closer look. Two of the ships had already made port. Amazing I thought, I wasn't expecting the ships so soon and never thought for them to stop on the docks. I was suddenly shoved and noticed it was some man calling me out in front of a large group of people.

"You don't belong here; you're not from Avalon. We never have had strangers in our midst because they normally turn out to be some sort of enemy."

Some people that had heard or noticed the confrontation turned to watch for my reaction. Really, I meant no harm and this was starting to aggravate me because now my view was blocked and I couldn't see a thing.

"Please, I don't want any trouble here, I am only interested."

"Interested people usually go and stick their nose where it doesn't belong."

"I only wanted to watch and see what happens; this is history in the making."

"You need to leave now before you make me any angrier and I'd have to make a scene." He looked heated already.

I replied, "Do what you must, but I'm staying and watching."

As I turned a few of his buddies surrounded me into a circle. They were all dirty and hadn't bathed for a few days from what I could tell. All of them were a lot larger than me. They were laughing and teasing and when I tried to walk past the one who started the brawl he pushed me. I dropped my belongings and that's when he swung the first fist at me and I ducked below the swing and punched him into his stomach. He swung back and then I punched him in the face. He fell to the ground with a bloody nose, which I was assumed was broken, and two of his friends jumped from behind me onto my back. I then kicked one in the shin turned around and fought both of them, pushing them into the ground. They looked up at me with surprise and hesitated to get back up. People who were cheering turned and started watching me fight. I weaved through the crowd with four men chasing behind me. All of a sudden there was a man in armory standing in front of me with a sword. He had bright blonde hair and he was in his late thirties. The men behind me caught up.

"What's all this?" The man asked.

"He's a traitor, he's not from around here; we think he's a spy," one of the men behind me suggested.

"Are you a spy?" The captain looked towards me and questioned.

"Of course not, I only traveled here to study and admire the city."

He noticed the damage I had done to the other men all by myself.

"You sure can fight then, yeah?" He then threw me a sword. "Fight me; let's see what you can do." Was this some sort of entertainment? By this time everyone around was interested in our quarrel and surrounded to watch.

We started our foot work inside the circle of villagers. He had a grin on his face as though he was enjoying himself. I started closer to him and made the first swing. This went on for a few minutes or so, only the sound of our swords clashing together.

"You have excellent foot work to not be a spy."

"I am not a spy," I said again with frustration. I knew nothing of sword fighting other than playing around with my friends with sticks when we were younger. And once in my teens I fought a boy who was picking on Dara. I found out back then I was a decent fighter and had to admit to myself that moving around with this sword felt very natural to me. The man looked well experienced and impressed. I hadn't the slightest idea what I had gotten myself into. The fight started to grow more intense. I knew he was serious. I was sure he had planned on killing me whenever he got the chance. We got caught into a bind wrapped together with our swords twisted up close.

He hesitated, "Do I know you? Who are you?" He asked me and then stumbled. I didn't respond back. I knew I didn't know him. Maybe he was trying to distract me. I knocked him with my elbow which surprised him. He stumbled down and the bullies behind me jumped me to hold me down just in case I was about to kill him. One knocked his fist in my mouth and I spit blood from my busted lip, angry at the whole scenario. This unnecessary confrontation was more than likely going to get me killed. The blonde soldier stood up looking down into my eyes with some sort of confusion and then lifted his

sword in front of me. Just before he was about to swing a man yelled, "Stop!"

A white haired man came across a path of all the other bystanders and he asked what was going on? The soldier tried to explain, but the man looked down at me, not listening to a thing the soldier was saying and staring fiercely at me without a blink. He then held out his hand, which stopped the soldier from finishing his sentence.

He looked down at me in some sort of shock and, with a whisper, said, "Is it really you?" I was stunned by his reaction. Who did everyone supposedly think I was?

"What is your name?"

"No one ever calls me by my name. I grew up with a farmer who always called me boy, so I named myself. My name is Alick." This put the elderly man in great spirits and he held out his hand and pulled me up rejoice- fully. The soldier looked back and forth from me to the older man in a dazed look and questioned,

"Alick, is it really?"

"Do you not remember us?" the older man questioned me again, never taking his eyes off of me, still stunned.

"No I am sorry; you must have the wrong person."

"See pa it's not him."

"Nonsense he looks exactly like he always has except shorter hair and a little older, come quick with us we will explain everything and fill in your blanks; this was to be expected."

By now over ten ships were anchored down in shallow water close to the nearby shore and a few people had come off to walk around on land and visit with some of the people of Avalon. I listened to the soldier and the elderly man speaking back and forth with one another and again I hadn't the slightest clue who they thought I could possibly be. They somehow had the same idea of who they thought I was. I finally brought up the courage to interrupt and ask what was going on.

"You are the warrior we have been searching for now for over twenty two years."

I huffed, "I'm only twenty two years old; that doesn't make any sense."

He turned and faced me, "Alick, you must remember who you are. I am Emeth and this is my son, Cadman. It may take some time, but I'm very sure you will remember us again soon enough."

He then explained that I was the boy from the stories I had heard of as far back as I could remember and went on about all the lost details that were missing. Damion left all of his power with his unborn child and his son refers to himself as Damion the Great. They had escaped the city that night after leaving me to face the army that had been chasing after them. They were on the run for some time after until, finally, a safe city, helped shelter and hide them. The last place where they had found refuge, Emeth made a new friendship with the king there who had leant them twenty ships to seek out Avalon's allies for war and someday return to Avalon. They had had twenty years of peace until two years ago when Damion's son picked up where his father left off, and it was time to go to war again. He unleashed his great army, which built great numbers over time, and they had been in hiding ever since. After filling in the blanks I assumed they were trying to tell me they thought of me as this lost soul they were going on about. I kept quiet, listening, fascinated by the man's story.

"Don't you think it must be true since we found you again and, out of all places, you were here in Avalon?" He asked me and I gave no response, but I questioned his words in my head. The story could be true if I believed in magic or immortality. Just yesterday I was planning on proving immortality wasn't real. He could tell I was holding in his words and thinking hard about it, enough for my head to begin to hurt, so he let it go for a moment to help it sink in, "We will have plenty of time to discuss these things with you later."

"You mean I am coming with you on board the ship?"

"Of course you are. I am not letting you out of my sight again, God so help me."

7. A Love To Remember

We sat down into a small boat and rowed up to one of the larger ships, and, once I stepped on board the vessel, I knew I never wanted to get off. This was where I belonged. All I cared for was sailing on this ship and I would say whatever it took to stay on board as long as I could.

"Cadman, go straight to the princess and spread news of this to no one else. Have a ship bring her further down the coastline so she can back up our proof."

There were only a few men on board and we soon set sail. Even though I had never been on a ship before, growing up, I studied everything there was to know about them from pictures in books. I told the elderly man if he let me stay I would be no trouble for him; I only wanted to help and sail the ocean.

"I hope you plan on staying a while, the princess sure would be thrilled," he replied and gave me a strange look, hoping to see some sort of a reaction from me and then looked out at calm sea waters and the miraculous view. 'The princess', the thought had only just dawned on me. I had been so distracted with the ship. Would I actually get to meet the princess? This sure had turned into a very interesting day. After a while we were further down the coast and rowed back to an unknown shore, except this time, no one was around and the beach was heavily secured with private guards. A ship followed from behind us. I went with Emeth for a short walk on the shore. I could tell he wanted to pick my brain. He asked me questions like, where I had grown up and had lived all this time, and I explained to him I had never met my parents and had lived with a farmer and worked hard for my entire life with only one dream to sail at sea someday. I ignored some of the ways he spoke because I didn't want to hear another word about me being a lost soul or any other non-sense idea about the topic whatsoever. I didn't want to hear it, so I made up my mind and I didn't hear. I only came to Avalon wanting to hear the stories, not be a part of them. Still the old man continued on with his questions of curiosity.

We talked for a few minutes then headed around a corner. It was beginning to become a little foggier outside with a chill breeze. There were a few rocks that I almost tripped over a few times. The ocean waves met the land and covered some of the rocks on the ground that we were stepping on, leaving them slippery. And then from the corner of my eye I could see a long light white dress waving in the wind before me. And there she was. I looked hard, squinting, to try and see her face. She walked towards me, but because of the fog, I could not tell what she fully looked like from this far away. She was walking impatiently faster the closer she came and drew slower when she was close enough for me to finally see her face. Our eyes met. The woman looked as though she was around the age of twenty four. Almost instantly I had a gut feeling that it was never Avalon I was searching for. Instead, she was the one who I was waiting to find for my entire journey. I had a flashback from my dream of the young girl who was standing on the beach and here she was standing right in front of me just as I had imagined. In my dreams I could never see the girl's face; it was always blurred out, and I thought she was much younger. This young woman's face was more beautiful than I could have ever imagined.

"Alick," she yelled springing into my arms! She looked up at my face, backed away for a second unsure of something, and then reached out to hug me again and I couldn't resist hugging her back. Instantly I felt welcome and affection. Quite an introduction to a princess I would have to say. Like all the others she seemed to recognize me.

"Walk with me," she said.

Cadman was muttering something in the background to Emeth about how he didn't approve of me walking alone with the princess. Emeth brushed it off and the princess paid no attention to what he had to say. We continued walking away from them for a private conversation. I was very interested in what she could possibly have to say after everything else I was told.

"Do you know who I am?"

"You're princess Irena. I've heard stories of you from my childhood. I believe everyone knows who you are."

"Do you remember who you are? Listen to me good Alick. You must know me, it is of great importance that you remember who you are and your purpose."

Princess Irena was not in her forties like I had originally suspected. Maybe there was some type of magic after all and more truth behind the legends. I admitted to myself I didn't want this to be real. Everything they had said to me wasn't what I expected to hear and a bit scary to me, so I took in the facts and tried my best not to believe the possibilities as she made her side of the argument sounding very convincing. She explained her case and then I said as sweetly as I could, "I wish I could believe what you are telling me, but I do not believe it."

This whole time, my life had been empty and lonely. I had spent years feeling as if something were missing and the first explanation I rejected it not knowing how to recollect the information retained. I was frightened of the answer so I ignored it. The princess let a tear fall. She came very close to my face, reached to touch it, and then she said, "I have searched for you for nearly twenty two years. Love conquers all. Come back to me my sweet Alick." She leaned in and kissed me. In the corner of my eye I could see behind her in the distance Emeth staring at us in wonder and Cadman turned his head to give us privacy or perhaps he wanted to ignore the scene altogether. And then I gave in and concentrated on the sweet kiss given to me and was completely into it, lost. The kiss was better than anything I had ever imagined before, and it felt like what I had been longing for and what I had yearned for my entire life. The feeling that couldn't be put into words, however, needed no explanation, there it was, the spark. The spark I had been waiting for. The spark I wanted to feel by a real kiss; the one that I never got by kissing Dara. I had been a mess for years with a lost broken soul. In that moment when we were together as one I swear I thought that time stood still. Anyone breathing who could dream up the most wonderful thing in their mind couldn't compare to this kiss. I was so eager for it from every ounce of my being. I wished that everyone could find this happiness once in a lifetime. The spark traveled straight inside my heart on top of the large gaping hole of emptiness and sadness and filled it up entirely, completely whole again. We stopped and looked at each other once again except this time it was different, I recognized her.

"Irena," I whispered ashamed of not remembering her at first sight. As though a light had gone off inside my head, I had suddenly remembered. Not everything. Some was still hazy. But I knew her and I remembered how much I loved her. She wrapped her arms around me and cried intensely into my shoulder.

"I knew it was you. I've waited for this day for so long."

"We found each other," I told her. "Do not cry."

"I am only crying tears of joy and happiness." I held her tight. "You look exactly the same as before," she told me.

"I guess I do."

"Well, except this time I'm older than you," she said nudging me and giggling happily.

"I'll catch up," I assured her.

"It's time to go now," Emeth called.

And we all left to walk back to the ships, Irena and I hand in hand.

Over the next hour we discussed the options of traveling back to where they had all been staying for the past few years in hiding, a small waterfall that lead to a secret passageway unknown to many people and secluded. They explained it was safe there and only a few days out at sea to travel back. There was also the option of staying a while longer at Avalon. Our people were the only few local people left and no one for many years had ever traveled into the city except for this past week, when I did. Staying here a few days shouldn't hurt anything. However it wasn't safe to make it permanent until Damion the Great was gone for good. It was only a matter of time before Avalon would be the first place he would come looking for Irena. All of these years Irena had never been back to Avalon, only to pass by when traveling. We decided to stay for a while just to celebrate my homecoming. I spoke to Emeth who brought me up to speed with updates and news of the so called, "Damion the Great." Cadman kept to himself and didn't look too thrilled that I had returned. Last time I had seen him, he wasn't even past his teen years yet, and now he was in his late thirties and a lot older than me. It seemed as if, and I didn't know for certain, he had developed feelings for Irena as well, which did not take me long to figure out by the way he was acting. Perhaps it was jealousy that he had for me after my return. That night, sitting by the fire with the old crew, I was reminiscing about all of the past memories from here at Avalon that I was now slowly recollecting. A few people told stories and then glanced over to have a look at me in amazement to see if I was following along and remembered exactly what they were talking about. Slowly but surely over the next few days my full memory came back to me and I could remember everything up until the night I had died.

Irena's beauty had grown. She was in her early twenties although she had the mind of a wise woman in her forties. She was smart and had bewildered me all over again. I was ecstatic that I had killed Damion and that she had been safe for all of these years because of me. Maybe I brought her some peace for a while. How hard it could have been for her that she had been alone for all this time without me. I felt bad for leaving her, and, now, she had gathered up most of her lost people and they praised her still. Most of her people traveled with her on board the ships. Only a few came back to the abandoned city after the war and would never leave Avalon as their home. I watched her walk through the village and speak to all of her people as if she had personally known each one of them and played with the smaller children of the group who followed her around. She was lovely. The next few days they celebrated my return and I enjoyed spending time and catching up on lost time and learning what all I had missed. I felt as though I had wasted twenty years of my life farming and slowly fading away with no meaning to it all. Now I understood why my life always seemed to feel empty and meaningless, why I had been so agonized with loneliness. Nothing could ever make me happy enough because, without Irena, my life had no meaning. It wasn't worth living without her. A couple days later everyone seemed to slowly forget I was there, like I had never left. I took Irena away for a long day alone. I couldn't imagine what this felt like to her, being with me again. I might have had a miserable lonely life, but she was lonely for twenty two years and knew exactly why. I had died. She felt every ounce of misery and grief and mourned for me every day since then. She had never stopped searching for me like she had promised. I loved her so dearly. She waited for me for all of these years. Being with her that day was one of the best days of my life. I was so glad to have her all to myself now, alone to catch up. We spent the whole afternoon talking, laughing, kissing, and I carved our initials into an old oak tree with a heart inside a circle. The heart represented our love that could not be broken or forgotten. The circle protected it. I traced her finger over it as she spoke about her experiences and the new memories she had made while I was away. I could have listened to her speak about her beliefs and love for her people forever and I did so for the rest of the day, which was nowhere near enough. As she spoke her incredible words of wisdom she amazed me in every way. I sat still for hours enchanted by her beauty, mesmerized by her lips, and listened to her intelligent wit, never interrupting because I didn't want to miss a thing. She spoke of the places she had traveled and seen as if she wanted to fill me in on every single detail since I had been away. She had lived a long adventurous life. I told her I wished I could have been there with her at all of the places she had described and then she told me that I was there with her - in her heart the entire time. I took in every second of her growing beauty since the last time I had seen her. She thought I was charming and just like that we had fallen in love all over again. I felt like the luckiest man in the world to have a second chance with my true love. True love always prevailed.

We were lying underneath the large oak tree that I carved our names into and all around us were fields of yellow flowers. Flowers grew instantly when Irena became close to them. Her power had grown immensely over the years. I couldn't help but take her hand and pull her to me. It was such a beautiful, wondrous day. We playfully rolled around together kissing, full of passion until she fell on top of me. I held her tight and could feel my own heartbeat against her breasts. Her face was exquisite. I quickly laid her down softly underneath me, kissing her as if it were my first and last kiss. Her breathing became heavier and made my head spin. I gently ran my fingertips over her soft skin. We had finally found each other, and we weren't missing out on this opportunity together now. That evening as the sun faded away and began to set, she didn't tell me to *stop.*

The next morning at breakfast I was the happiest man alive. Life had felt like it was just beginning for me again. I couldn't help but keep a smile on my face and I admit there was a certain skip in my step. I suggested we go exploring. Irena smiled at me from across the table. We had talked the day before of riding off to see some of the country side and how it had changed. I could tell Cadman was not happy.

"Exploring?" he questioned me.

"Hunting if you will," I suggested again cheerfully. "I'd like to make up for lost time," I continued.

"I'm sure you've done plenty of making up, haven't you!?" The comment was offending. Everyone became quiet and listened in for my reaction. I stood. He might have been older than me now and a little confused since my absence, but I was still in charge as before and no one ever questioned my authority. I was the leader for the king's army and I was back now. His comment was unnecessary and embarrassed Irena who was blushing to herself. He needed to be put in his place. I already knocked him on his ass before and now I had a slight bit of my memory back and wasn't wasting a perfectly good day with this nonsense.

"We ride first thing at noon!" I shouted. I stared straight down the long table at him, deep into his eyes man to man. I then remembered getting on to him for causing trouble when he was eleven. I could still see the fear deep within his eyes, as if he were still that same child from way back then. Just like nothing had ever changed. For many years he had proven himself worthy to lead, but now I was back. He didn't question me again he just rose up from the table, apologized to Irena, excused himself and stormed off.

Once he left I respectfully apologized to Emeth and continued to eat my breakfast. I knew Cadman had done a fine job in protecting the people and Irena. Maybe some things were different now. We went for a walk after breakfast and Emeth explained to me how the past few years had been hard on Cadman and, unsure if I would return, he admitted Cadman had grown fond of Irena. Emeth had warned Cadman not to get his feelings wrapped up too deeply since Irena was already spoken for. He tried all he could to impress her, only Irena never gave up hope of finding me and Cadman out grew her in age. Cadman might have an attitude and a short temper; still he had always treated Irena with respect and dignity. After I returned with some of the men from a successful day of hunting, I confronted him later in the afternoon. Once I learned of how much he cared for our cause and fought with his life to protect and serve Irena, I wanted to start off fresh and make things right between us.

"I knew it was you when I saw you," he said to me. "I didn't want to admit it to myself; I liked the ways things have turned out since you've been gone. I wanted Irena all for myself and deep down I knew I could never have her," he admitted. "She's been waiting for you, and you make her happy. So I will not get in the way because I only want her to be happy."

I put my hand on his shoulder and told him he was a good man. It couldn't have been easy to feel the way he did and I had admiration for him for putting Irena's feelings before his own. In other ways I have done and would do the same. We talked for the next couple of hours, not keeping up with the time, about how so many things had changed since I had been gone and how so many things were different now. He told me at first he didn't want me to be back here and it was hard adjusting to it. Now he admits he was just confused about everything. He always believed it all, but never truly accepted all of the facts for himself. Now that I was back it proved everything was true and he finally realized how serious the wars were to come. He was only a small child when we left Avalon and he never remembered how serious the battles were on that particular day, but he remembered how tough those years were that followed, always on the move. We settled things and knew we were both fighting for the same thing, Irena, which was the only thing that mattered to each of us. I even playfully joked around and said, "And you better never try to kill me again." I left him sitting on the balcony after thanking him for keeping her safe and all that he had done for her people. When I came back down to the refurnished rooms where we had been sleeping I was told Irena had left with Emeth who escorted her back to one of the ships. She had asked me to join her, so I started making my way down to her. I made a quick stop in the village market before everything closed and asked around to a few places for something I was looking for. Finally, I found something suitable, and continued down to the port. When I reached the ship I climbed on and Emeth headed back to the city.

"Why have you come back down to the ship?" I asked her.

"Well you were gone for a while. I waited for you, but the city seems so different now, not like I remembered it. Without my parents here it just seems empty sometimes. Since you have been away I learned to love the sea because I knew how much you loved it. I expected to live with you for the rest of my life so I thought I ought to get used to sailing." I rubbed my hand across her face and pushed the hair back that was falling in front of her beautiful eyes. She yawned.

"Come," I told her. She leaned on me as we walked down to her cabin where she slept.

"I have something for you," she said.

"Oh do you, I was about to tell you I had something for you, ladies first."

She walked over to a bench and lifted the top. Inside she pulled out a cloth and un-wrapped it.

I couldn't believe it, "My father's sword, how did you?"

"Your sword," she corrected me. "We have been several places over the years and I came across it. I paid some good money for it." I ran my fingers over the markings and thought of my father. I then made my way over to her, picked her up, and spun her around. "Your father would have been very proud of you," she assured me. I gently put her down and fell to my knees in front of her.

I leaned my head into her waist and then looked up at her and took her hand, "Irena, my darling, I love you so dearly. I promise I will always love you forever. Please marry me and make me the happiest man in the world." I pulled out a small silver ring with a pearl in the middle, the only decent ring I could find, given the circumstances. With tears she replied, "Yes," overjoyed! I slid the ring on her finger and then we held each other tight and for a while swayed back and forth in the middle of the room. At some point I finally picked her up and carried her off to bed. We made love again that night.

8. Into the Deep

Over the next few days we started packing up our belongings and preparing the ships to leave. We enjoyed spending time back there at what we considered our true home, but, like always, we knew staying there for much longer wouldn't be safe for us. A few men that had gone out hunting earlier that day had ridden back in a hurry and I went to see what the matter was.

"Quick," they shouted! "We saw some ships coming from the west, we must go now!" I gathered up the last of our things while Irena said her goodbyes to her people.

"We must go Irena."

Whoever was on the ships sailing towards Avalon mustn't find out the princess was here. She followed me onto the ships and as soon as we were aboard, the anchor was lifted we started to sail away. We both glanced back at the same time not wanting to leave, for this was our home. Our people never stopped waving as we sailed away. Irena shed a tear.

"We will be back someday," I reassured her.

"I'm fine," she nodded, "as long as you're with me." I grabbed her hand and kissed it. She continued, "I'm home with you."

We headed out East and into the blue ocean waves. I was finally living. Slowly my memory continued to come back to me and I began helping with every part of the ship. I enjoyed every bit of it even though others would call it work. They named me captain like my father before me and this was my ship. I gave orders and kept it clean.

Every person had their own part and daily routine. All I needed was Irena and my ship and I felt unstoppable. Irena stayed at the head of the ship mostly and only retired below the deck at night. I trusted everyone on board, but, just for a safe precaution, any food that came from the galley was tasted and checked for poison between four tasters before I would allow Irena to eat. She thought I was being over protective but never brought it up. I loved everything about her, even the cute smart smirks she would still give me when she thought I was being ridiculous or overbearing. I didn't take anything for granted with her.

Sailing was the same for three weeks until one foggy morning. It was a very rare occasion to see thick fog like this out at sea, and I knew from experience it wasn't a good sign when a sailor did. Fog was usually a sign of trouble or bad luck. It was hard to look out and see anything unless from up close. It was too quiet for my comfort so I climbed up to the crow's nest to see if I could have a better look out and spot anything of interest. If something were out there I wanted to know in advance so I could plan accordingly. I could barely make out our other ships and some had disappeared from my vision. I saw ripples in the water down below. Something very large was in the water and swimming around underneath our ship. I glanced down at the crew, including Irena.

"Get away from the edge," I called down!

Everyone backed up into the middle of the ship. Irena started below the deck. I yelled to her, "Irena stay up top and stand in the center of the vessel." I shouted to the men to keep a close look out and prepare the cannons in case we should have to use them. Only a few minutes later I saw it. Over the fog was a large sea serpent wrapping itself around one of the other ships, almost breaking it in half. I had seen many kinds of sea monsters before in my life and knew where there was one that usually meant there were more. I signaled quietly to Cadman and told him to tell the rest of the crew not to make any noise. I could the see fear in everyone's eyes as we all heard the screams and cries coming from one of our other ships. In the back of my mind I was thinking we could fire canons over to hopefully hit the sea serpent, but then it may sink our ship. There was a chance we hadn't been spotted yet and could out run the sea beast. I climbed halfway down to discuss options with Cadman.

"What is it? What do we do?" he asked urgently. I explained this particular kind of sea serpent was attracted by noise. Somehow we had to get a message to the other ships to get away from this area as quickly as possible and figure out a way to save our people from sudden attack. Cadman went up to the crow's nest to wave a flag and signal one of our ships over. The closest ship to us arrived in less than a minute.

"Emeth get them away as safely as you can."

He looked at me as if he thought I was crazy.

"There's nothing we can do!" he exclaimed.

"We can't sit back and watch and not do anything. We can't leave them here like this!" He asked me what he could do to help.

"What you have always done, your best. Protect Irena. Get her away from this danger, so I will be able to concentrate on what I need to do and nothing else."

"We just got you back," Irena interrupted. Then with a slight pause she grabbed me and said selflessly, "Do what you must." She knew there would be no negotiating with me on my decision and that I was made for times like these. Since the beginning, my soul instilled in me the power needed to always protect mankind no matter what the sacrifice. Irena understood even though she hated to risk losing me again. Half the men boarded the ship beside us including Emeth, Irena, and Cadman even though he adamantly refused. He wanted to help, but I would not allow it. He needed to stay with them in case anything happened to me. Then they would need him, especially Irena. I wouldn't have her lose both of us, the only men who truly cared for her. Cadman had brought them this far without me, and he was their best shot. Should anything happen, I felt like they adjusted well enough the last time and could surely do it again.

Irena held her head down and turned away as the ship started sailing away. She couldn't bare to watch as I sailed out toward the direction of the sea serpent. As soon as the ship was nearly out of sight from the fog, we concentrated on the desperate ship in need. Our ship turned side by side to the other, "FIRE," I yelled as the cannons pulled and accidentally hit the ship instead of the serpent, trying to miss the ship. I could see several people had jumped or fell into the water trying to escape. Finally, one cannon's blast hit the giant sea serpent and it fell back into the deep ocean waters, but not before pulling what was left of the ship down under with it. Just as several men shouted in victory, another sea serpent rose from out of the water and wrapped itself around our ship. This one was much larger than the first. Its body was scaly and shiny like a snake and had the head of a dragon. I couldn't tell where the body ended as the tail was tangled around the ship and half still in the water beneath. No time for thought, with my adrenaline rushing, I instinctively charged the beast. The men followed my lead. We fought with all we had, but no matter how hard we swung, if we managed to hit the serpent, it hardly noticed the pain. Realizing this was going to get us nowhere, we would have to try something different. If we kept this up for much longer our ship would end up like the first one. I noticed a young man distract the sea serpent by striking its tail with a sharp weapon. As soon as the head came towards him, I jumped on the lower part of the back of the sea serpent's neck. The serpent made a sort of hissing sound and it suddenly jolted back down into the water with me hanging on its back. Under the water the body of the beast appeared never ending. I held on tight since I knew I was around the area of the head and didn't want to lose it. Part snake and part dragon I knew the only way to kill it would be to either chop off its head or pierce it through the heart. Since the beast was swimming quickly and deeper into the ocean, I did not have the breath nor the time to pull myself up to the head. So I took my sword and stabbed the serpent as deep as I could, not actually knowing what part I was stabbing, but I was sure it was somewhere around the neck. As the beast slowed down in pain I turned around to the front side and drove my sword down into the sea snake again and again exhausting the last of my energy. I could see straight into the beast's eyes as they closed and the body drifted slowly into the darkness below. Out of breath, I started swimming up to the light. I knew I would never make it; I was already too far down and starting to suffocate. I could see the ship above me thankfully still intact. I knew I had done what I needed to do and had fulfilled my purpose. With no energy left to keep on swimming, I gave up. As I started to drift away I saw something in the distance swimming towards me. My vision was blurred. At first I thought it was Irena. Then she touched me. I looked into her eyes and she kissed me. It wasn't Irena. And then I figured it out; it wasn't a kiss, it was air. I looked around. Mermaids. The one giving me breath had white blonde hair, with gold and pink shiny scales, reminding me of Irena. There was another nearby with pale skin, jet black hair, and a blue tail. Another I noticed was freckled skin and had a red tail with matching hair. These were exotic and mystical creatures. Another peculiar mermaid with silver hair and shiny scales suddenly came up to me and gave me yet another kiss of life. I was surrounded. I knew nothing of mermaids except the old wives' tales I used to hear from fishermen about how mer people lured men into the deep sea with their magnificent voices. They had no intention of hurting me; they saved me. The one with gold and pink scales pointed down to the bubbles rising from the dark and blew a conch shell. I assumed she was trying to thank me for killing the sea serpent and then, with one last breath, they swam away and vanished into the deep blue ocean.

I started swimming up. As I rose to the surface my hope was rising with my body. The men on the ship called out to me in astonishment, "Look there, he's alive!" I heard one say as he pointed. They pulled me up and I climbed on board, falling to the deck exhausted. I lay there for a brief moment, catching my breath as the men gathered around and looked down at me. One of the older men pulled me to my feet,

"How did you?" he asked. "Are you alright?"

"I'm good," I replied with a smirk.

"Count your lucky stars," he said as he turned and started cleaning up what was left of the ship. We had many survivors on board that swam to our ship for safety. The fog was almost gone now.

"Let's go find my princess now shall we?" I started to inquire the damage. The damage was not that bad, and only a few things needed to be replaced or fixed. They had already picked up all of survivors from the other ship wreck. My clothes were almost dry by the time the fog finished lifting and we could see the other ships from afar. After staring attentively I could make out there was a large number of ships from in the distance than what was our own.

"Let's hurry over, quickly," I demanded, unsure of what was happening.

This had me extremely nervous. Impatiently I was pacing back and forth. They were still too far to tell whose ships they belonged to. The unknown was concerning me. 'God, please let Irena be alright.' I thought. Suddenly I became the most frightened I had ever been in my life when I saw the sails blowing in the wind were black enemy sails. Pirates had already raided and taken over half of our ships, and we were one of the last ships left to stand and fight. But we were unprepared. The others stood down unsure of what to do. What did they want? Pirates only took over ships for treasure. And we didn't have treasure, only trinkets, weapons, food, and Irena. They had easily taken over and captured most of our ships, including Irena's. The pirates and the crew were only standing around watching our ship come quickly forward.

"What's the plan?" I was questioned by some of the men.

"Prepare for the worst and draw your swords." Looking over at our other ships that were surrounded, it seemed, like they didn't know what to do. Irena's ship was already taken over and she was captive. We kept our distance in case they tried to take over our ship as well. Our ship may be the only chance left for escape. I needed to think of something brilliant now and act fast. We couldn't fire for risk of damaging our own ships and harming Irena. Looking around at all of my useless options and our captured ships grouped up together, I noticed familiar faces looking at me waiting for some sort of signal. Most of the men were ready and able to attack at any second given any order or notion.

The pirates had taken over most of our ships, which didn't leave us with great numbers, compared to their own, which left an uncertain outcome that I was beginning to fear. When we were close enough to see what was actually going on the first thing I searched for was Irena. She was standing alone with pirates surrounding her, but she was alright. Cadman and Emeth were close by her and surrounded as well. Cadman looked vanquished from being hit from what looked like several times. The chances of us fighting and winning were slim. I carefully thought out my options. We were side by side with Irena's ship and the head enemy vessel was on the other side. Irena's ship was stuck in the middle between us both. We anchored there, but kept our distance. Before making what could be a deadly decision I wanted to see the pirate's reactions, to see if I could determine what they were after. Pirates were known for violent robberies at sea. I have had many run in's with pirates before and this was not typical of them. Never had I seen this few in a group able to take over such a large number of vessels in such a short time. It was unusual, almost as if they were looking for something specific. 'Maybe if we offered them food and whatever else they wanted we could part and be on our way without confrontation,' I thought to myself. I was willing to divide the ships willingly if it meant my crew's safety. Pirates were usually only violent when they needed to be. They were still busy raiding Irena's ship. The violence had already happened. I was sure the worst was over and that we could strike some sort of deal. I cared for nothing on board any of our vessels except the people.

"Stay here and guard this ship. If any other ships come over pull out, with or without me. We need this ship intact in case there is no other escape route for Irena." The men asked me what I planned on doing. I explained how we might be able to negotiate something with the captain before any of our men had to get hurt.

"Be careful. Pirates are liars and unfair." I was warned by the crew, and was sure of it. That's when I noticed Irena's hands tied behind her back with rope and her mouth covered. She was being shoved and taken over to the enemy's pirate ship. I wasn't having it. I swung over on a rope and landed on the deck of our main ship as Irena crossed over the plank to the other. Immediately several pirates came at me with swords and I took each one down. I chased after her on the long plank to the enemy vessel, and when on board a large pirate put a knife at her neck.

"Not another step!" he threatened.

"I wish to speak to your captain to negotiate a settlement." I pronounced. They all laughed obnoxiously hard. Again several pirates came at me with force and I put each one down one by one with my sword.

"I can do this all day," I said and meant it.

With a grunt he said, "He wishes to speak with the captain."

It grew silent and everyone stared in my direction. I turned and looked behind me and there he was, coming out of his chambers, and I wasn't for sure.

"What would you like to negotiate?"

A man my age who I knew instantly was dark within appeared.

"The girl and the crew go free and take as many ships with them as possible. And in return we don't fight back and we give you whatever you wish on board any of our ships." I grew weary, looking into his dark eyes. Those eyes I knew. I had seen them before. Fear started to rise inside my chest.

"I can see you're very brave," he paused and for a second I thought he was agreeing with me and then it struck. That horrible pain I remembered. I had felt it before; like lighting pouring out of him and into my body. Suddenly I landed on the cabin floor. Irena screamed, "STOP!" At least that was what I thought I had heard come out of her and then the pain wore off. Two pirates came over and grabbed me up. I could no longer stand on my own and my whole body was still in agony.

"I understand that you killed my father," he continued. He looked at me with disgust. "This means the princess is very valuable to me."

He walked over to Irena and stared at her improperly. "Shhhh," he whispered as he uncovered her mouth and ran his fingers down to her chin.

"Don't touch her," I could barely let out.

"My greatest power and weakness standing right here in front of me," he said to her doubtingly.

"It's me you want. You have been looking for me your entire life and your father before you, and here I am. Let my people go free and I will go with you willingly."

Everything happening in front of me was hazy, but I tried my best to pay attention to every detail. The way he looked at Irena was how I have seen several other violent men in the past look at her this way before. It disgusted me. He had horrible intentions for her, I could tell, and now he was completely obsessed with her. He grabbed her face suddenly, which frightened her. Then he announced, "This girl is no threat to me. I was going to keep her prisoner and torture her to keep her weak so that I would live forever and fulfill my father's dreams before me, but now I see what would truly hurt her the most." He walked over to me. I was almost back to normal as I looked up at him again. "What am I going to have to do, princess? If I kill your lover he will only come back in a different life for you. Wait, I have an idea. What if I keep him prisoner and you can watch him suffer every day and grow old without you? And then when he dies, I would have lived a long enough life and then kill you too, right before he returns to find you dead."

"NO." Irena was in tears. He was taunting her.

"So when he comes back to find you again, it will already be too late. You'll be dead and I can kill him again and again and he will have to live forever without you. I believe that gives me around three lives to live. Plenty, I'd say. And you," he turned to me and whispered what only I could hear, "After seeing your miss pretty princess over there, I think I will make her my wife and take her to bed with me each night and then maybe turn her over to the rest of my soldiers when I'm finished." I tried my hardest to go for him with what strength I had left in me, but his men held me back and he struck me again and I hit the floor. He laughed. "Let's see, what else could I do? What if I had a child with her? I wonder how powerful my son would be if he had both our powers combined." He was saying everything he could to get underneath my skin and it was working as I lay there not being able to do anything about it, almost lifeless.

He thought for a moment and said aloud for everyone to hear, "Let the men go on their way and the princess stays with me." He then whispered something in one of his men's ear, "Send a ship after them and when they aren't expecting it, kill them all. The princess won't resist as much if she sees we let her people go freely." They both laughed.

He nodded and started dragging me to where I assumed I couldn't escape. I knew they planned on torturing me. My ears were still ringing, but I heard Emeth calling out to me.

"Alick must go with the other men," Irena demanded. Damion the Great did not respond to her and the men kept dragging me forward.

"I said let him go!" she yelled and light flashed around her and she broke the rope bounding her hands together. This now had his attention.

"Well I'm glad to see you do have some power after all my dearie. Look men she can break through rope, good to see you're not worthless." I tried to reach out for her and the closest man to me kicked me in the stomach. She ran over to me. All of the men were standing around watching us, laughing.

"You underestimate me," Irena said furiously looking straight into Damion's eyes, fearless. Everyone grew silent waiting to see what would happen next.

"We shall see!" he said with anger and excitement. Just then almost in a blink of an eye, both of them shot out their powers at one another and fought. I had never seen anything like it. Everything seemed to be in slow motion. The light coming from Irena was brighter than the sun itself and so blinding to the eyes that you couldn't look into the brightness. It filled the air from all around, and the lighting from Damion met hers, an even brighter light shown in the middle where their powers had met together. I had never seen Irena use her power like this before. It surprised me that she was capable of something so magnificent. What she had possessed here was a little piece of Heaven although darkness had come. Her light over shown his and over powered him. When it hit him he flew to the other side of the ship and he hit the ground. It seemed to affect Damion the same way his power had affected me and he was shocked. Irena then struck everyone around us and we started to escape. I was limping and she was helping me. Emeth and Cadman started fighting with the rest of the men. Some of our ships had a head start. I knew Emeth wasn't leaving without us. My life was flashing before my eyes. We were running to the ship, and it seemed close enough to reach out and grab. I drew my sword and turned to face Damion. He was now standing and looking at us both wickedly. He wanted a hateful revenge; I could see it in his eyes.

"Irena your power is stronger when you're with me. Now is the time to try. Your power over powered his. Good will always defeat evil. Let's keep fighting."

"What if I'm not ready?" she questioned.

"Irena, listen to me. When I am gone, do not cry. Everything will be alright. You will be in my heart wherever you are. When destiny calls you, you must stay strong. You've got to always stay strong. I may not be with you, but I will be in your heart always."

"I can't live without you Alick, not again. Life has no meaning without you," said my beautiful Irena.

"Then fight with all you have." I kissed her, and turned. We were standing side by side facing him, this time together.

"What are you doing?" Emeth called out. Damion shot out more of his energy and Irena blocked it with her light shield, his power never touching either of us. He stood there for a second and I could tell he was questioning his next move. He wasn't expecting her to be so strong. Even though he took a second before striking again I knew he would do so soon because he didn't want to seem weak to his army. He shot out all that he had once more at us and Irena was now struggling to keep it back. She was running out of energy. It was too hard for me to see her this way, I couldn't bear it, so I did the only logical thing any man would do for the woman he loved and went for Damion myself; not knowing if her power could still reach to me from that far away from her. I had no choice. I wasn't sure what was going to happen, but I knew he couldn't fight me and her, too, at the same time. The closer I got to him the more her light ran out of my shielded area and I realized I was vulnerable and no longer protected. He might strike me with his dark power, but not long enough to kill me. He was preoccupied fighting off Irena. He saw me coming at him and knew he had to do something. Just before I almost reached him to strike him, he lifted one hand and made a portal in front of me that I fell into. It was like a quick jolt and then I fell onto land. I quickly looked around and there was no ocean. There was no one in sight. What was this place? Some sort of trickery? I swung my sword all around in case he was still in front of me but I couldn't see.

"IRENA," I called! What if his portal sent me somewhere else? 'How do I get back?' I thought as I was pacing back in forth in panic. Irena was fighting him right now and I wasn't there. I didn't know what was happening. I tried everything, even walking back through the invisible portal that was no longer there. What was this place? It was very dark and gloomy here. I had landed on grass and there were broken stones everywhere around me. A place of ruins and every second that went by the clouds were rolling in and making the sky darker.

After a few shaken minutes I started walking around and thought maybe I could find another way out of whatever this place was. Standing around in the same place wasn't going to help anything at all and I couldn't waste any more time. What happened here? Looking around more I noticed that some of the land had been destroyed, which looked like only recently. And then I saw a beast fly over my head. I held my sword up, startled. The dragon breathed fire in the air and roared as it flew through the hills. I ran to follow it. Why didn't the dragon attack me? I kept running for it, being the only thing I had seen yet. I continued to follow the dragon until it was almost out of sight. I saw smoke coming from the ground in front of me and I headed towards it. Swords were clashing, and men I had never seen before were fighting from all around. The ground was nothing but ash. The site looked like the end of time. The creatures fighting the men were frightening. Some had large animal faces. Large magical creatures were fighting alongside the men. Wild creatures I had never seen before - Giants, Centaurs, Minotaur's, and others I didn't recognize. One of the very large Minotaur's ran for me and I struck it down.

"Alick," a centaur called out to me, looking as confused as I was.

"What are you doing? The tower," He yelled!

As he pointed and looked up at it and the dragon flew over it. He somehow knew me and I was taking this as a sign that I was supposed to be at the top of the tower. So I started running for it, through the battle, taking down anything getting in my way. Inside I heard the most terrifying sound - Irena's scream of pain. I paced as quickly as I could toward the horrific sound. I found her in a room. There she was lying on the ground out of breath.

"Irena what happened? Are you alright? Say something," she looked up at me stunned and in a shock.

"Alick, How?" she asked surprised.

"I don't know what just happened, my sweetheart. One second I was on the ship watching you fight Damion and the next second I was here. Tell me what has happened."

"Oh I see," She was gasping for breath. "There isn't much time to explain Alick." She was weeping. "Damion is here, coming for me any second. You went through a time portal somehow, and this is the future." I tried wrapping my head around that thought for a brief second.

"I don't know how long I've been gone Irena my love, but I'm going to keep you safe. What good would I be to live a thousand years without you?"

"Oh, Alick,' she wept. "How I've missed you so, my guardian angel. There isn't any time. Just know that I love you so dearly with all of my heart, more than you can ever even imagine or even begin to grasp." I gave her a quick kiss and stood to face him again.

"He's coming, I can feel it," Irena said.

I drew out my sword and stood still, waiting.

"Hide, he's not expecting you," she said.

I stood behind a stone column. The room was large and the ceiling was tall. The floor was made out of stone rock. I heard noises coming closer.

"Where were we Irena?" It was Damion's voice. I couldn't believe it. 'Was she his prisoner?' The thought made me sick.

"You were just about to finish me off, but now I have something I didn't have before," she replied.

"What is that," he sneered.

"Hope. I know now that everything will be fine," Irena responded.

He sighed, "Irena, you're losing another battle outside, and I am about to finish this once and for all. I'm afraid there is no hope for you." He was about to lift his hands to kill her and I jumped out to swing as he let out his force onto her. She let out the last jolt of her energy left within her, which only blocked the impact for a second. I swung the blade deep inside him as he pressed the rest of his power from her into me. Her light hit him very hard, which immediately brought us both to the ground. As I lay there looking over at her still, lifeless body a tear fell down my cheek and I soon drifted away and died for the second time.

PART 3

9. A Soul Dead

The darkest of days were upon the world. Sadly I had experienced it firsthand. For many years I was a servant and I grew up helping soldiers with the dark army. As a boy, I adapted and lived the only way I knew how - doing whatever I was told, which sometimes meant watching them kill innocent people and not doing anything about it. My life felt stuck in one place and could go no further. There was nothing I could do and I hated it. My heart grew cold, my self-esteem lowered, and I was turning into a hateful bitter man, dressed like the soldier that I despised. I thought of myself as a murderer, robbed of my life. For miles stretching on the earth beneath my feet was nothing but ash and a constant battlefield. "I have to get out,' I had been telling myself for years. Now was my only chance. It was late and the guards were drinking and soon to pass out from their drunkenness. I untied one of the horses and snuck out into the night. It was not going to be an easy escape. There were eyes everywhere, always watching and waiting, but if I were stopped and questioned, my plan was to say I was on night watch double-checking each post. I imagined this escape for so long. 'It could work,' I convinced myself. If not I could be free from this place, which was the same as death. I was old enough to be trustworthy, as much as one could be trusted around here. I had always kept to myself and remained quiet unless called upon to do something. I acted like I was clumsy because I didn't want them to know I actually knew how to fight for fear they would call me to do more with the army. I acted invisible and so I was. The only decent thing I had done in my life was I once hid a family from the soldiers as they burnt their house to the ground. At least they lived. That was the only decent memory I had of myself. Just in case I was caught I decided to not get on the horse just yet. I walked slowly so it didn't look suspicious in case I was being watched. I had seen many men try to escape before on different occasions and they were always struck down and killed for trying. I had only seen their leader Damion in person once before and hoped I would never have to again. He sent chills straight down my back. Something that day made him stop near me and I kept my head down because I didn't want to be noticed. Thinking of him again made me quiver. It was a face you could never forget.

All of the horrible memories I had from my past kept flashing through my mind as I made my way past the gates and towards the woods. It took many years to finally build up enough courage to try. When I felt safe enough, I climbed on the horse's back and rode off into the night, as fast as I could, fearing for an arrow to go straight through my back at any given moment. I kept riding all through the next morning with all that I had, never thinking of stopping. My life depended on it. I was so terrified of what I had just done that I didn't plan on stopping until the horses legs had given out. It wouldn't be long before they noticed the horse was missing and figured out who was gone. Then they would send some men to finish me off. I spent the next three days going on like this, turning around, looking over my shoulder to make sure no one was behind me, completely paranoid. The slightest noise in the forest spooked the horse and had me on high guard. The creature must have felt the same way, I was sure. The smallest movements made me draw my sword. My mind had grown mad with paranoia. I wondered how I wasn't found by now, which surprised me. My God, it might have actually worked, I thought. I could be free. I waited for this day for so long. Oh how I waited my entire miserable life for this day to come, unsure of what to do now that it had. I had seen so many terrible things for way too long. The nonstop killings of war agitated my soul. I had horrifying nightmares every time I slept, always waking up in a sweat. During the day the images haunted also. The things they had done. What I had seen. I knew I was ruined for life.

Finally in a few days' time I could actually see green grass again and the surroundings started to look normal. The land was usually dead wherever I traveled or I was taken. Things were looking up for me for once. I might actually have a chance. It was a cloudy morning and I noticed a small river. I stopped by and let my horse have a drink and rest. Rest was something I wasn't used to. I noticed smoke rising from the other side of the creek. I tied my horse to a tree and decided to sneak over and see what it was in case I was in some sort of danger; maybe the dark army camping out searching for me.

One of the traits I had picked up on with the dark army was learning how to be quiet and sneak up on people. Lying there asleep were a couple of men who looked like they were hunters. I grabbed some of their clothing that they had hung up on tree branches to dry from washing in the creek and then snuck back out. I stripped off my soldiers' armory and quickly bathed, putting on the new clothing so I wouldn't be recognized. I knew I didn't want these hunters or any other person in these parts of the woods seeing me and thinking I was a soldier of the dark army. If I wasn't killed on the spot, I would be tracked down by many others. I tossed the outfit into the river, untied my horse, and rode off in the opposite direction from the men. The clothes were baggy, but I somehow tied them all together to make them fit well enough and thought I had looked half way decent, not that it mattered. I wouldn't be seeing anyone for quite some time unless I wanted to die. My hair had grown long and I had a chin full of scruffy facial hair. My facial hair was thicker than it had ever been before, and grungy enough to look as though I belonged to the forest. I needed a good clean shave.

I rode for several days until I reached a small village. I decided to go around so I wouldn't be noticed. I liked to keep to myself. The only friend I had ever made was a boy, named Nathanial. He was one of the few soldiers that tried to escape from the dark army and was tracked down and killed. I hadn't been found yet, but that didn't mean they hadn't stopped searching for me. Death became something I was no longer afraid of. I suppose I thought of death too often and somewhere along the line stopped caring. In fact I felt as though I deserved it somehow for all of the bad things I had seen and done in my life. The past days alone made me reflect. Sitting back and watching someone do harm to someone else is just the same as doing it to them yourself. I should have been killed a long time ago. That's how to survive in this world. I had never cared for anyone other than my friend Nathaniel and, after he died, I taught myself that feelings and emotions were a sign of weakness. No one could break me. I was too tough. Sometimes I wondered if I even had a heart or soul. I felt lost; however I refused to ever be that man again. Alone in the forest was where I thought I deserved to be.

Winter was coming. The nights grew colder as the days passed by. I could not risk building a fire and being found, unsure if there were any soldiers still hunting me down. I knew it was probably only a matter of time before they did track me down and kill me. One clear day when I went hunting deep into the woods it started snowing lightly. I spent a few hours carving out an arrow head that was attached to a wooden spear I had made to throw at my next chance of supper, whatever that might be. My stomach was rolling because I had been starving. It had been more than two days since my last meal. A squirrel was the only thing I managed from the last hunt. Food was scarce these days. At this point I honestly didn't care if I ate a rat; however I had hope for a small rabbit. I sat a couple hours in a tree listening for any sound or movement that I might hear. Just then I saw a hog moving in the brush. I climbed down quietly. I had a good arm, but I needed to be a little closer when I threw it. I didn't want to miss this time. My hunger depended on it. When I was right up on it and before I started to lift my arm back to toss it, an arrow came quickly over and went straight through the pig. I stood back behind the closest tree I could find and looked in the direction the arrow had come from. Hopefully I was not spotted. An older teen boy with dark curly thick hair was on a horse. He was facing me and when I realized he was alone I walked out from my hiding, making myself known. He saw me first. He seemed nervous not having expected me and lifted his bow as I put my hand on my sword. "Halt," I exclaimed. His arrow would be faster than my sword, but I was quick and sure that he would need to use at least three to keep me down by the time I might already have my blade pierced through him. That was if he was a good target, assuming so since he had the pig.

"What's your business here?" the young man asked me.

"Well, you killed my hog." I said jokingly.

"Your hog?" he questioned.

"My supper actually, but I suppose you plan on killing me now too?" I asked with a sarcastic grin. He put down his bow.

"I guess I could share the hog. There's plenty of meat," he offered. "What are you doing out here in these woods hunting alone?" he asked.

"I guess I could ask you the same question. I live out here." I explained.

"Live out here by yourself?" he questioned in disbelief.

"I like to keep to myself." I acknowledged.

"My name is Theo, what's yours?"

"Alick." He glanced over quickly and said, "No kidding?"

I asked, "What?"

"Unusual name that's all."

We started slaughtering the pig and agreed to split it equally to share.

"Say, I have a long travel ahead of me, could I crash with you tonight?" he asked. "It's better than sleeping out here alone and besides I can help you build a fire."

I nodded, "Sure, why not?"

I had to admit it was nice talking with someone.

The fire was warm and I quickly swallowed my food almost without chewing. When my stomach settled, I continued to try to figure Theo's personality out.

"What brings you through these parts of woods? I hardly see anyone travel this far, or, better yet, alone, especially a young lad like yourself?" He continued to chew his food as though he was thinking too hard for an answer, but nothing suspicious to make me question him any further. "I only ask because you seem too young to be hunting out here."

"Where does your allegiance lie?" he asked.

"Like I said before, I keep to myself and care for nothing else. I'm not into politics." He looked up at me and seemed to be questioning himself whether to tell me something or not. Then he asked, "So you have no beliefs or opinions of your own for this war?"

"No," I replied.

"Well, I'm on a mission for the princess and Avalon's people. Twenty of the best men were sent different directions to call on our allies for more help. I'm heading east to round up some others. It is time to stand and fight. The time has come." He was rambling on and I listened carefully.

"You keep east and don't dare go west," I suggested. "The dark army is there." He knew I was helping him now.

"Wait, you've seen them?"

I nodded, "And you're supposed to be one of the top soldiers the princess has to offer?" I questioned him in disbelief and the comment seemed displeasing to him.

"Look, I know I'm young and small, however, I did get this position somehow and, not to sound cocky, but offend me like that again and I'll show you what all I can do." I could only laugh. His little threat didn't scare me at all. "Keep laughing," he pouted.

"It seems to me, if you were one of the best, you wouldn't tell a complete stranger about your secret mission." He was young and naïve and only rambling because he was proud and liked to brag. I've seen his type before. Then I thought hard for a moment and couldn't figure out from exactly where I had seen that type before. Something about the boy was familiar to me. The fire died down and he rolled over and passed out. I was unable to sleep with the arrival of my new company. I wasn't used to ever having anyone around me. Even though he was only a boy, I never trusted anyone while I was sleeping. The entire night was uncomfortable for me, always in and out of sleep and ready to jump up to kill with any sudden noise in the forest that I heard. The next morning as he was preparing to leave on his horse, I filled his bag with enough meat packed with snow to last a couple of days for when he grew hungry.

"You should come with me," he suggested. "Of course, not if you're going to toss and turn and talk in your sleep every night." I never knew I talked in my sleep before and it made me nervous to think for a moment about what exactly I had said.

"Safe trip young Theo." And just like that he was gone.

10. A New Friend

I continued my usual routine over the next couple of days or so. I hunted, slept, and tried to keep warm at night. Only once did it come to mind that maybe I should have gone with him on his quest. Not to help, but to make sure he got to where he was going safely. Maybe doing some things right for a start could make up for some of the horrible things I had done in my past. Then I thought to myself, 'No, nothing could.'

I went out the next morning to hunt. I ventured out about a mile further than I normally went and, as I sat up in a small tree, I heard some horses galloping nearby. I looked up and saw Theo on his horse coming towards me from around some hills. Right after him was five soldiers from the dark army. I quickly jumped down and onto my horse. I rode over to him as fast as I could. The forest was thick so I knew Theo was heading straight into it to try and lose them. As he headed into the forest, I passed right by him. I was going in the direction of the soldiers. He saw me and yelled, "What are you doing?"

It was already too late.

The army had seen me and recognized me at first glance. I now had all their attention. They had me hedged in between them from all sides. I was surrounded.

"Let's settle this then, yeah? You're best man against me." They resented any sign of courage. I knew they planned on killing me even if I won against whomever came over to fight me first, which happened to be the captain of the group, Bigon. I knew him well. He was the leader who killed my friend Nathanial years ago and now I wanted revenge.

"We've been looking for you. I'm sure you know, of course. The question is, how did you manage to escape us for so long? And did you really think we wouldn't eventually catch up to you? Look men," he boasted. "This one actually came straight to us," he sighed. Then they all laughed. "Your little disappearance almost cost me one of my guard's heads, you know?" He raised his sword and I drew mine also.

"Now, I'm going to kill you and send yours to Damion as a gift." He swung at me and our swords clashed together. When I was in the dark army, I had always followed his direction with my head held low and my lips sealed. He thought of me as a coward because before, I never stood up for what I believed in and that's the only thing that I ever regretted. I fought like I had never fought before. I wanted to show him that this was the last time he would have any sort of effect on me. We stayed tight together, both struggling. He started sweating after a while. The other soldiers just watched and waited. I was getting tired and knew if I killed him, I could never finish off the others by myself. He would swing and I'd duck. He came at me with full force and continued to push me until finally I was pinned against a tree. What he didn't know was that I had seen his battle tactics in the past and watched him closely for years; planning, waiting for my chance. I would let him go on with full strength until he thought he was winning.

"You're stupid for ever trying to leave us. Damion is the only future for this world."

"You're wrong," I argued.

I pulled out my hidden dagger and shoved it into his stomach. Shocked he stumbled to the ground and I raised my sword to finish him off. The other soldiers got down off their horses making their way towards me in anger and complete surprise that I had beaten their captain. I was completely surrounded. Everything happened so quickly. And just when I thought this would be the end an arrow came from the trees and pierced straight through one of the soldiers. More arrows came down shooting in from all different directions. I looked around, but the forest was too thick to tell how many were shooting at the soldiers. One by one they fell and I quickly took the last one down. I heard some crushed leaves from somebody walking towards me and a limb break when out from the trees came Theo.

"Who's with you?" I asked.

"I don't know what you mean?" he looked at me surprised.

"You mean to tell me that you shot all of those arrows just now, by yourself?" I questioned him, still not believing my own eyes.

"I told you I was one of the best."

He had a small grin on his face.

"That was so quick, how did you?" He stopped me before I could finish asking.

"I've been shooting a bow ever since I could hold one in my hand. I thought if I led the soldiers into the forest I could lose them once inside and then, when they split up searching for me, I could then take them down one at a time."

"Well then why did you wait until the very last minute when you could've just shot them the entire time? I was trying to help you. It didn't look like you had much of a chance when they were chasing you."

"I know. I just wasn't expecting you to ride straight up to them like that and, after what I witnessed I was enjoying the show. I wouldn't have let them kill you, of course. What was that all about anyway? They acted like they knew of you from somewhere. How?"

I'm not sure why, but I decided to tell him, but I couldn't look him straight in the eyes when I spoke the words out loud. My head held shamefully down as the words spilled out unexpectedly easy.

"I use to be one of them."

Completely mortified at what he could be thinking of me as I told him the truth. Theo was the first person I had ever talked to that wasn't a soldier and who could possibly understand. As soon as I looked up he already had his arrow raised pointed at my direction.

"A soldier?" he asked me again and I nodded. "For the dark army," He was still in disbelief.

"Yes," I admitted, completely guilty. "Shoot me if you will. That seems the only proper punishment."

For reasons unknown to me, he dropped his bow back down and told me that we needed to move far away from this area as quickly as possible as more would come looking for the missing soldiers and that I could tell him more of my story along the way. Theo looked at this advantage as an opportunity to learn more of the dark army for his cause. I explained how over the years I had learned the dark army's tactics and I could teach him their ways of operation. He was eager to learn everything that I knew of them. He tried as best as he could to listen to the horrific stories I shared without judgment. Theo carefully listened to every explanation of my story with as many view points as possible.

"Do you suppose there are others like you there, trapped, unable to leave?"

I told him of Nathanial. We stayed up late that night as I told Theo my story of how I was born, raised, and brought up to become a soldier for Damion's army; That every moment I had endured I had despised and ended up hating myself for being a part of it for so long. He somehow seemed to understand as best as he could, but he was also wary since he had never seen a soldier from the dark army that was a good hearted person. My story intrigued him.

"We mustn't speak of this to anyone else," he explained. "If people knew they would try to kill you."

"Maybe I should be killed," I stated back.

"No, I believe there is a reason you made it out alive and you need to figure out what that reason is, not waste it," he suggested to me. "I've known you for a while now and I can tell there is goodness in your heart whether you can see it now for yourself or not." He was innocent and perhaps a bad judge of character. We spoke for a while longer and then retired for the night. As we awoke the next morning he told me I must come with him and that I could trust him. He gave me his word he wouldn't tell anyone else of my secret and convinced me to help him on the rest of his journey since I did owe him my life.

We traveled for days until we reached some caverns that lead to another village inside a hidden forest. The forest was enchanted with beautiful waterfalls and colorful flowers I had never seen before, and beings I had never even heard of. This is where Theo explained that we had many allies, most of which were creatures not human, mainly Centaurs. They were men on the top half with the lower body of a horse; very brave and gentle creatures. They protected each other with their lives and were very loyal to one another. Women and children Centaurs were the most important thing to the men. Their leader was named Agrius. He was known for his skills in hunting and knowledge of medicine. Rarely did a centaur die because of the medicines they knew how to conjure out of herbs for various wounds or sicknesses. We stayed there with them for almost a month until we heard news of other allies traveling back to the princess's army and preparing for the Great War. During my stay there, I learned a lot about life and family. I learned things I never had gotten to experience on my own. The younger centaurs played together with their fathers and as I watched I eagerly yearned for the same relationship for myself someday, however I hardly thought I could ever deserve such a thing. Agrius and Theo would go hunting with me in the mornings. We would compete on who would get the first kill. It was the best time in my life. After I learned a bit of Agrius I could tell we were a lot alike; neither of us liked to show our emotions. When we left the village I could honestly say that I could call Agrius a wise and noble friend of mine that I knew I could trust. Trust wasn't a feeling I was used to. And while most of the Centaurs whom I called friends would travel back with us to battle, I knew I would miss it here and everyone I had met over the past month. When the war was over, I planned to travel back to this place and make it my permanent home. This was the first thing

I had found in my life that I loved. For the first time life had meaning to me.

The centaurs were the only family I had ever known. All the men in our group seemed like brothers to me. While traveling over some very dreadful areas on our way to join the princess's army, we killed several soldiers from the dark army and fortunately never lost a single man of our own. Centaurs were excellent fighters. I felt unstoppable, like I had a reason to live. I wanted to destroy the dark army like all of the others. I finally found my purpose. Protecting the good men I was fighting with was my destiny, and I would easily lay down my life for any one of them. I especially became close with Agrius and Theo. Theo was like a son I had never known. Agrius was like an older brother to me. He taught me a lot of things during my stay. I was told we were only a day's walk from the beginning of the royal border. We were about to enter the princess's territory. There were guards lining the border protecting her lands. If someone were to manage and get passed the guards, there was a magical shield blocking the border. Nothing evil could get inside; only the pure – hearted could enter. This made me nervous. What if I could not go through? We were met by some of her guards. I tried not to make it a big deal in front of them as I stepped over the force shield expecting something to happen. I went through surprisingly. The guards led us the rest of the way and we followed close behind them. They seemed in a great hurry to return to hear the princess's proclamation, which would be in the morning. She would officially announce the plans of war and the city was celebrating her coronation. She was becoming queen tomorrow afternoon. No one in the group wanted to miss it. Hopefully we would arrive early enough in the morning in time to see. As we crossed the border it was getting late in the evening. I noticed there were great large stones, similar to tombs that reflected as a mirror would. I couldn't tell if it was actually stone or made of something else.

"What are those?" I asked Theo. I thought they were graves.

"Those are magical portals," he explained as we were walking past them. Supposedly no one was sure exactly how they worked. Only great magic could open them and sometimes people can be sent through them.

"Where do they lead?" I asked anxiously.

"I guess anywhere - the past or present and anywhere in the world." "Impossible," I responded.

"I've never seen it happen, of course, someone actually go through one, I mean, however we were taught about them growing up. Those stones have been there for thousands of years. The princess's advisor studies them."

I thought they were very interesting.

The places we traveled and passed never ceased to amaze me. The portals were very peculiar to me. He brushed it off like the portals were nothing. Finally we arrived. The city lights in the distance were a sight to see. When dawn's first light lit up the city, my eyes were astonished. It was the largest city I had ever seen and, unbelievably, beautiful. Nighttime was just as beautiful with all of the lights, but in the day, wow! It was just after first daylight when we reached the gates, which surrounded the entire city. Hundreds of homes were inside and the castle towers were in the center, which inclined. The higher you climbed the further you could see out over the walls. The army was huge. Thousands of men surrounded the walls; archers like Theo, who were above the walls and always ready for an attack. On top of the mountain the highest towers looked so tall that the tips were almost touching the clouds. All of the leaders were inside the castle, planning the arrangements of war and preparing the battle tactics. The guards rushed us in so they could get back on city watch. For now we were stuck inside to do whatever we wanted so Theo showed me around. There were many different shops and market places. Each home had its own garden or space for something useful to grow. The people made a living by trading goods and certain food and animals that they raised.

11. The Coronation

The horns blew and the princess stepped out of one of the tallest towers and looked down at her people as they gathered and cheered. She waved and smiled. She was beautiful, in a white gown, although it was hard for me to see her from the far off distance. I could tell she was passionate for her people. They were well supplied with whatever they needed, and I could tell that the people here were happy and each person loved her in their own way. She waved and walked back inside. The coronation would be soon.

"Merek," Theo shouted! Another lad headed over to greet us.

"How are you Theo?"

"Great!" Theo introduced me to Merek and gave him a quick pat on the back. He said he had to go prep some armory.

"Good to see you again Theo. We should catch up tonight."

"Sure thing. Tell my grandfather I've returned please, whenever you see him."

"You never told me you had a grandfather?"

"He's important here. I don't get to see him that often. He wasn't too pleased that I volunteered for that last quest. He'll be glad I'm back, and I'm sure he'll send for me whenever he gets around to it. You can meet him then." Theo showed me his house. It was ordinary like all the others, but the inside was very unique. It was like a museum; tons of ancient weapons and artifacts that surely could have made him rich. He had a ladder that climbed up to a loft where he slept. We spent the rest of the afternoon catching up on some sleep because the coronation had been postponed for a few hours. Finally, it was time to head to the palace to celebrate the princess becoming a queen. Most everyone stayed outside in the palace streets. It was very crowded and loud from all of the commotion and people cheering. The princess would walk out onto the balcony above the crowd with a crown after she became queen.

"Come on," Theo shoved me. I followed him inside the palace gates, confused.

"Can we be in here?" I questioned.

"The guards didn't stop us, did they?" He always had a smirk on his face. I always thought he was up to something. I also noticed he was a hit around town, very popular, and had his way with the ladies, always with a cheeky deposition.

"There you are my boy," an elderly man with a white beard was walking over to Theo, his grandfather I assumed. Some women standing close to Theo walked off giggling as the men stood around speaking of non-sense, which I learned was what most men liked to do here when they had nothing better to do. Since I had always been alone with no friends to occupy me, I had to quickly learn the dos and don'ts to fit in around here. My communication skills were awkward. I was unfamiliar with proper gestures. To my surprise everyone in the city was quite friendly when meeting me for the first time. Agrius snuck up from behind me and we started talking.

"Grandfather I'd like you to meet..." and then the horns blew. The speeches began and Theo's grandfather walked off in a hurry. Theo whispered, "Sorry, you'll meet him. I told you he's just busy." I felt important. We were inside the castle with all of the men of honor who lead the army or made major decisions for the city. Theo had snuck me in here somehow, and I felt grateful to him. There were blue and red flags hanging all around. Whenever there was an announcement gold horns blew. Everyone in the room was either on the left or right side, leaving the middle space with a red fabric rug that traveled all the way up to the throne. The throne was made out of gold with perfectly designed patterns. There were seashells engraved on the chair where the queen would sit. Beside the throne, Theo's grandfather was standing, holding the gold crown on a soft silk pillow. Several people spoke about the princess and how honored they were to have known her. She led the people so strongly and gracefully. And after everyone was finished with their speeches, the horns blew and the doors opened. And there she was, walking out of the side doors and upon the landing next to the gold throne. She stood there for a second, looking out at all of her people. Her dress was made out of an off white lace, so elegant it reminded me of a wedding gown. She was quite lovely. And to think I was once fighting on the dark army's side against her. Why would anyone want to harm this beautiful, graceful, and perfect young lady? Everything she had done for her people was selfless and good. I could tell without even knowing her that she was worth fighting for. All of the stories that had been told about her had blown me away and there she was, in person, standing right there in front of me. She had very much inspired me to be a better person. She gave a perfect speech about the war and how we were as ready as we would ever be, although I hardly noticed what she was saying. I was still mesmerized by her beauty. Then Theo's grandfather went up next to her and spoke about all of the years he had known her and how proud he was of her reign. He spoke of how the coronation was a symbol of a young girl coming of age to rule. He said he was ashamed to have waited so long to celebrate her, but, as everyone knew, they had never really had the time with the war. He was blessed to have been fighting for her. He held up the crown and slowly placed it on her head.

He then announced, "Presenting for the first time, Queen Irena." Everyone bowed down to honor her. Since I wasn't aware of these proper gestures, I was a couple of seconds late to go down to a knee. And so when everyone else went down to praise her, I was standing alone in the crowd. Her eyes met mine and stared, not leaving my gaze.

"Emeth," she whispered as she fainted and fell to the floor. Everyone stood up frantically as Theo's grandfather went down by her side. He shouted for help.

"Someone bring water." Her eyes were open and she was saying something to the man that no one else could hear. The man was looking around the room while whispering to the queen.

"The queen is fine everyone," and he helped her up. "However no one leaves this room until dismissed." Everyone was looking around at each other unsure of what was happening. The queen sat down on her throne and Theo's grandfather started walking around as if he were looking for someone. I kept myself hidden because I had a strange feeling he was looking for me. Why did the queen faint when her eyes had met mine? He turned back to her, "he's not here my dear."

"He is! I can feel it." she snapped back while holding her head. He kept pacing around the room and then went back to her, "Maybe you should retire early to your room. You're just overwhelmed with everything going on right now."

"I'm not leaving this room and neither is anyone else until you find him. He's in here, and I can feel it." They were whispering back and forth. No one knew what was going on or what they were speaking of. Everyone looked confused because no one could hear the conversation between the queen and her royal subjects. Some were even frightened that their queen had just fainted. Then the old man started pushing through the crowd again, looking at every face. It was only a short moment until he found me.

"Everyone must go now except for my grandson and his new friend here." The queen looked as though she had a headache and her arm rested her head as she was looking down from her throne. People started leaving, whispering amongst themselves. I was sure that now was the time for me to start running. She must have known somehow

I was once with Damion's army. Maybe she knew things like that. I was sure I was dead.

"What's this about?" I questioned Theo, "I'm not sure either. It's fine. Trust me." He kept reassuring me as I started to panic. Surely Theo didn't give up my secret, I thought to myself.

After every person left, the older man spoke, "Theo, my grandson, where did you find this man?" I watched Theo carefully, wondering what he would say. Theo looked up at his grandfather and said, "In the woods, several months ago. I was on my way to gather our last group of allies, and he was hunting. We met and he saved my life from a group of dark soldiers a few days later. We became friends and then we traveled back here together." The queen's servants tried to hand her another soaked handkerchief for her head, but she refused.

"I want to see him," she demanded. One of her guards took her by the hand and helped her to her feet. She walked over to me staring attentively. By the look on her face she seemed delighted, perhaps even joyful; she smiled for a second. I didn't understand. There were guards standing in front of the door, the only way out. For some reason I was very nervous. Things were very quiet for a moment.

"What is this all about?" Theo finally asked.

The older man spoke, "I am Emeth, Alick. Can you remember me at all?"

"How do you know my name?" I was very confused and after a minute or so it somehow clicked for Theo.

"No way," Theo was stunned and looked over at me, "Alick." He wasn't sure what to say, but something seemed to make sense to him as well. I was still out of the loop.

"Does someone want to explain what's going on to me? Am I supposed to know you?"

All four of us including several guards must have been in that room for many hours and I lost track of the time. Still trying to make sense of everything they had explained to me of what they thought I should know. Emeth tried to explain what had happened to me, but I did not remember any of it. There was no memory of anything they were telling me. I was told it had been almost forty years since they had last seen me. Emeth was the queen's most trusted advisor and loyal friend. He was the closest to her for years and they explained to me that that was why he hadn't aged from what I would last remember of him. The queen had kept him younger. He was a reminder of her father to her and she wasn't ready to let him go. They explained how I died the last time as the ships had been taken over and the queen and Damion fought. I had tried to strike Damion and with both of their powers combined; he somehow pushed me into an unknown portal. After I disappeared through the portal, while Damion was distracted, the queen struck him one last time and the ships evacuated while he was down. Theo was intrigued by the stories. He had only heard small parts of them before so this was a first for him also. After half the night had passed we all agreed that it was time to retire for the night. It had been a very long day for us all. Queen Irena had let Emeth do most of the speaking. I don't think she was sure of what to say, although she stared over at me most of the time, curious of how I would react to what they were saying to me. I knew of queen Irena from the dark army. All of these stories were new to me. I had never heard of what actually happened to her. As we were leaving the room to head back to Theo's the queen invited us to stay in the castle for safety reasons. I wasn't sure either one of them were letting me out of their sight. I waited at the door for Theo as his grandfather whispered something to him.

"Watch after him and I'll do the same for the queen." My head was throbbing as servants walked us to our new chambers. Theo was quiet until we were alone in our room and then he suddenly became ecstatic.

"I can't believe it! This whole time you have been Alick from the legends I've heard all my life. How did I not put two and two together? And of all people, I'm the one who found you!" He noticed I wasn't really saying anything in return. "Hey, I know it has been a lot of information for you to take in this evening. I'm still pretty stunned myself. If you want to talk about it we can, but if not we don't have to right now."

I nodded, "I think I just need some rest now, I'm quite tired."

"Very well. I'll leave you to it." He walked over to the door. Our bedrooms were connected. I went over and stood before the fire lit in my room. In the doorway before he turned to leave he said, "We can finish talking in the morning," as if he were almost certain that I wouldn't want to talk to him then either.

It was a restless night with lots of tossing and turning. I was unsure of what to make out of all of this. I had a thought that everyone now had expectations of me to be this good, brave, hero that everyone adored. I quickly became ashamed because I was not the same person. I thought about my past, the dark army, everything. How could I live up to my own expectations? And then there was the queen in love with me, waiting for my return for almost forty years. How could she love me? I thought about all of the responsibility I had now, living up to my name, comforting someone I hardly knew, being someone I was unsure of how I could be. I felt unworthy, a feeling I knew very well. My insecurities attacked my mind and swallowed me for the rest of the night.

The next morning the servants brought breakfast into my room. Theo knocked like clockwork. We ate together. Best friends who were unsure of what to say could sit together for hours and not say anything at all. We were just comfortable with each other's presence. We didn't need to have some long conversation to understand one another. He knew how I was feeling and I wasn't ready to talk about anything yet so he let it be. Trying to change the subject, he talked about some girl he met the other day and then realized that was only making me think of queen Irena so I suggested we go hunting instead after our breakfast. Theo knew me well; hunting was something I could do. Hunting would keep my mind distracted from everything going on and I needed a break from my thoughts. I needed to clear my mind to refresh my soul.

We had a very successful day of hunting quail. Agrius tagged along but left later in the day. Theo and I didn't return to the castle until almost nightfall. Emeth was outside waiting for us at the gates.

"Is something the matter?" I asked him.

"No, no it was just getting late," Emeth replied.

"Are you my wife?" I said jokingly.

"I told you he worries too much and is over protective of me," Theo said.

"You ought to be glad someone cares for you Theo," Emeth replied.

"Plenty of people care for me, grandfather, and now that you've reminded me, I have to go meet one right now." Theo winked and was off.

"Alick, I'll be back in a bit to help you skin the quail. Don't start without me," his voice trailed off and he was gone. Emeth and I had an awkward staring contest for a few moments. He finally asked if he could walk with me.

"You thought I wouldn't come back, didn't you?" I asked him.

"I knew you had a lot to take in and you've been thinking hard about it all day whether or not you want to admit it to yourself. It has been almost forty years. I told Irena, that this time was different. It would take some time for you to get your memory back, if you ever did at all. I think she has accepted it, but I'm pleading with you to take in consideration her feelings for you. The only thing that matters to me now is that she is prepared for what she must soon face. She needs to stay focused on her enemy. Better late than never for your return, but I do not want her getting distracted. It's not the right time."

He told me queen Irena wanted to speak with me earlier today, but learned I was gone. Since we snuck past the guards, no one except the stable boy knew we were gone. Emeth said he waited outside the gates most of the day, hoping I hadn't fled. He said he had spoken with Agrius when he returned to find that we were only hunting.

"Look," I said, "Whether or not I am this person you speak of, I am a free man able to make my own decisions. I stayed because I wanted to be here. I want to help fight in the war and make sure Theo stays safe. I can't have everyone concerned about what I do with my days while I'm here."

"Fine," Emeth agreed and said, "I wasn't sure what to expect, however I am glad you are back." He turned to leave. "Goodnight, Alick." It surprised me how such a wise man listened to how I felt and trusted me. He thought he knew me, but no one did.

What a day, I thought as I walked into my chambers to find Irena pacing back and forth on the rug in front of my iron bed post. She looked up realizing I had just walked in. "I'm sorry for startling you," she apologized with a stutter.

"How did you get in here?" I asked.

"I have my ways. I didn't want anyone else to know I was here. I just had to see you for myself."

"Queen Irena, look, I'm not,"

"Shh," she interrupted, "you don't have to give me any explanation. We don't have to talk about anything now. I just had to see you in case you were leaving."

"I'm not going anywhere." She was gazing at me, "Good, I'm glad to hear it." I don't think she was sure of what to say. I had no memory of her. We didn't really have anything in common that we could talk about. Things were quiet but not awkward. She walked up to me, staring right into my eyes. She reached out and touched my face with her soft gentle hand. Something about her was familiar, but I couldn't figure it out.

"I'm so glad you're back now. I've waited for so long."

She looked as though she desperately wanted me to kiss her and for some reason I wanted to kiss her, too. I couldn't explain it. I stopped myself because it would be wrong for me to kiss her when she believed I was someone else, someone that I was not. I was a stranger. Would it be wrong if I kissed her only because I thought she was pretty? Not pretty, that wasn't the right word and beautiful didn't do her justice. Just then, the door opened and Theo was standing in the doorway with his jaw dropped from seeing us both there, together.

"Uh, sorry guys. I'll come back later," Theo interrupted.

"No, it's fine, I was just leaving," queen Irena grabbed her shawl and walked to the door way passing Theo. "Goodnight Theo," and she turned to look back at me, "Alick." I nodded and said, "Goodnight." Theo watched her leave, astonished. Slowly he turned his head back to me with his mouth still open wide, waiting for an explanation.

"What was that all about?" he asked, bewildered.

"Don't look at me like that Theo. I wasn't expecting her to be here either."

"Well, well already playing catch up. Way to go buddy."

"Theo *stop* it," I huffed. "Ok, I guess I'm ready to talk about it now."

"About?" he asked. I thought I needed some advice.

"Well, I've thought about everything long and hard, enough to make my head hurt really bad and I guess what it all comes down to is, now what? I'm not really sure what I'm supposed to do and if I truly accept the truth. If I am this Alick that everyone thinks that they know from a different life and I could get past that and accept all the facts, what am I supposed to do with it? I know nothing of this person. I cannot be him even if I tried to and I have a feeling everyone expects this person from me sooner or later. Everyone thought I was going to walk away today. If I hadn't spent all of my time with you today, who knows, maybe I would've left."

"Why?" he replied.

"Because one, it all sounds a bit crazy, and, two, it's a lot to live up to, you know?"

"I guess, I mean I can understand your perspective with everything you've been through." he responded.

"I'm not leaving. That was never the plan. I'm staying to fight against the dark army. That was the original plan and is why I came. I'm doing this for me, no one else." Maybe everything would fall into place, I hoped. Theo agreed.

"Well, I'm not sure what will happen, Alick, if that's what you're afraid of, but you should know, I believe that maybe this was the reason you escaped the dark army to begin with. I believe in you, the person you are now, not because of what everyone else thinks of you, but because I knew you had a big purpose when we first met. The person you are now is just as good as the one you were before. I'm sure of it." He started laughing. "Sorry, it's a little weird when you think about it. I wish I could come back after death."

"I'm not sure I'm ready for any of this." We talked for a few more hours and played a board game by the fireplace.

"She's so beautiful," I said out loud.

"Irena," Theo asked?

"The queen," I replied.

"Indeed she is."

"I don't see what she could have ever seen in someone like me. It's been forty years. I can't even fathom being young for forty years and having lost someone I loved for that long of a time, knowing they would come back without remembering you and just sitting there waiting for their return.”

"Yeah,” he agreed but barely paying any attention to me as he made a fantastic move on the board.

“Has she been with anyone?” I asked him.

He looked up at me and said, “The only person I know of is you.”

“Don’t you think if I had had her I would remember something like that?”

“You would think,” he smirked.

“Alright it’s late, I’m turning in.”

“Awe come on, I was winning.”

“My head isn’t in the game or I’d be beating you.”

“Fine then. Good night, poor sport,” he yawned and walked out.

The next morning Theo and I went out to the marketplace to meet the maker of Theo’s bow and arrows called the Artillator. Theo was an archer and expert marksman. After he picked up his new toys, I went to watch him train ten new crossbowmen. After a couple of hours, Theo and I practiced hitting some targets. We were both competitive with each other, but I had to admit he had me beat on shooting targets. His aim was perfect every single time. He almost never missed the red circle in the middle. I watched with amazement and I was impressed at how anyone could have such a great talent, especially at such a young age.

“Well, you were blessed with other things. You can’t have everything,” Theo teased me. “Good show. Let’s call it a day.” We ended the day around supper time only to find the entire village was celebrating inside the castle. Upon entering the castle we found queen Irena and Emeth walking toward us.

“Go get cleaned up you two. We’re having a grand celebration in Alick’s honor,” Emeth announced.

“This isn’t really necessary,” I said.

“The queen insists.” I looked over at Theo, “You knew about this?”

"Someone had to keep you busy for the day." I went with him to get dressed for the special occasion. There were outfits laid out for us in our rooms.

"I don't need some huge celebration Theo." I was forcing myself to get dressed and trying to convince myself it would be alright. The whole idea made me feel uncomfortable. Everyone would be focusing their attention on me for the night and I wasn't anywhere near ready or prepared for it. In fact, it was my worst fear.

"Come on Alick, this will be good for you. Just enjoy it," Theo said.

When we were done getting dressed, we stood looking in a mirror at how nice we both looked. I had never dressed in such proper clothes before. It was almost too fancy for my taste. 'I actually look half way decent,' I thought. And of course Theo was rubbing it in.

"I don't know about you Alick, but I sure am good looking." I shook my head at him as he stood in front of the mirror.

"Let's go Theo." I guess it was time to do this. I was so terrified of putting myself out there and getting hurt somehow. My fears sank in. I really needed to let go of what others thought of me. It was a constant battle in my head every time I talked with someone new. I was always thinking about what they could possibly be thinking of me as I spoke. I tried so hard to convince myself that I could do this. I could be the person every one needed. Every time I built myself up with confidence, my doubts would kick in, attack my mind, and put me back into my actual place, which was a cruel reality. I knew somewhere deep inside my core that I was made for a great purpose and I came close to the realization that maybe it was to protect the queen. Everything had lined itself up perfectly without me having to do anything. I guessed that was what true fate felt like. These people did need me; however, I was unsure of what I could give them. Almost as soon as Theo and I walked into the ballroom crowds, came up to seek out a conversation with me. Most were women of nobility, who were some of Theo's old flings, wanting to meet me. One in particular was Lady Jezebel, who flirted with me constantly. Theo finally stepped in and pulled me away. I took a deep breath, "What took you so long? I nearly suffocated in that crowd from perfume."

"Better stay away from that one," Theo warned. "And better soak it in and get used to it." Theo continued, "This is how it is with royals, nothing but gossip." For a second I wished to be anywhere else at the moment and then I saw queen Irena making her grand entrance and I suddenly changed my mind. She was being escorted down the lined steps and onto her throne. She had on a tight, white lace gown that looked elegant. The dress she had on at her coronation was made for a princess; this gown was made for a queen.

I couldn't believe my eyes. She was almost too beautiful for my eyes to look upon. She didn't look real. Her hair was braided, long with little flowers parted on the side. I couldn't describe her beauty if I tried. Across the ballroom she sat on her throne. I had to go speak to her. She had many subjects visiting her from around the world. Everyone predicted we would be at war within the next month or two. All of her allies gathered here to feast and fight by her side. A line of guests had formed of to be introduced to and greeted by the queen. The line quickly moved up and, in front of me, was a handsome man around my age that stood awaiting his turn to meet the queen. There were two guards standing on each side of queen Irena for protection. His name was announced, "Sir Callum of Maldova." He seemed to have the queens' attention.

"Your majesty," he bowed and kissed her hand. She seemed flattered, but she glanced behind him, back at me for a brief second.

"How are things in Eurasia, Callum?"

"Just fine my grace. I am glad to be back to your beautiful countryside. We shall talk later, yes?" He asked.

"Of course Callum, as you wish, but when the proper time comes." I didn't understand what was being said, and it made me feel uneasy for some reason. He bent his head to show respect before he disappeared into the packed room full of dancing people. I was next. I knelt down before her with my head down.

"Rise," she said. "Come sit beside me please," she insisted. "Enjoy the feast and party, Theo," she called out to him and he was off. I never noticed him standing behind me. She had my full attention. "This is all for you, you know." She looked over at me.

"I'm not sure I deserve it."

"If anyone deserves a celebration, it's you Alick." She said back to me. "You have fought for me with all of your being and paid the ultimate sacrifice for it not once, but twice."

"I have no memory of that, or of you." I said. She looked at me as if she were hurt by my words.

"And because of your sacrifice you have lost yourself."

Emeth was standing in front of us now, "We should make the announcement now for our guest of honor, your majesty." We continued to look into each other's eyes for a moment, not hearing Emeth, "So our guest may eat," he continued.

"Yes," she agreed and stood. The music stopped and everyone in the room became silent.

"Arise, Alick," and she held out her hand to me. I took it and stood beside her. Emeth was on her other side. "Everyone here knows the truth of this man's story, who laid down his life for me many years ago. Some have grieved with me over the years. This feast is to celebrate his return tonight, a feast for the man on my right, Alick of Avalon!" Everyone started cheering with continuous clapping. "May we win this war, have peace return to our land, and someday soon be able to call our natural country home once again, with Alick by my side." She looked over at me and everyone cheered, even louder, including Theo who I caught in the corner of my eye. She held my hand and lifted it up in hers, "To Alick!"

"To Alick," everyone exclaimed as they were seated.

People seemed to be very much inspired by the illusion of our love. Listening to those cheers, I couldn't quite take in that they were all for me. It was only at that moment that I realized these people, from all around the world, truly believed in me. If I were from another life, I was once a hero and that I would have to start believing in myself in the same way. We sat back down to greet some more quests and watch the dancing. I glanced over at queen Irena again and saw something different this time - She loved me with all of her heart. I could see it in her eyes, and even though I had no memory of her from before, something was there between us. Before I knew it, instead of fighting for her side, I had made up my mind to fight for her. Not only would I make sure nothing ever happened to her, I would make sure we won the war. Somehow it just had to happen. I was unsure of where the sudden desires sprang from, but I would do this for her. I would do anything she asked of me. She was a queen made for ruling. I asked her to dance with me. She had a smirk on her face, "what?" "Dance with me," I said again. She hesitated again. I asked, "Are we not allowed?"

"Yes," she agreed as she took my hand. We swirled around the room as everyone watched, though for once I hardly noticed. I knew the music. I couldn't remember where I had heard it before, but I had heard it from somewhere for sure.

"We are pretty good at this. I've never danced before." She giggled slightly,

"Yes you have." I looked at her confused. "We have danced together before, once when we were children, and again, later, when we were hiding out in a cave," She stopped.

"I'm sorry I do not remember."

"Maybe one day you will."

"Perhaps," I nodded. Emeth interrupted and asked if he could dance with the lovely new queen. As he took over and they continued on the floor, I was yet again swarmed with another impatient crowd wanting to meet me.

"What is it my darling?" Emeth asked Irena as they were dancing around the ballroom. "Emeth, I can slowly feel him coming back to me." "Irena, even if he were to live three lifetimes, he still may never remember. It's going to be hard for him this time; he's been gone for quite some time."

She paused; "I don't believe it. I just can't." Upset she stormed off the dance floor into the crowded room.

I watched as they stopped dancing and watched her walk away from Emeth so I tried to hurry through the crowd to catch up to her. She disappeared into the crowd. I was looking all around the ballroom for her. Callum had grabbed Irena's hand, startling her and pulling her behind some curtains that led onto a balcony.

"Callum," Irena huffed, "What are you doing, If someone should see?"

"Well my lady, I couldn't help myself. I had to see you again."

"It's Your Majesty now," she reminded him. "And it has been for almost a year. I told you that I am not yours."

"I know. I just had to look at you one more time." Irena gazed up into his eyes as he was about to kiss her, but she pulled away.

"I can't. I told you, he's back."

"Just one kiss? Please love, for old times' sake."

"No Callum. You aim too high this time. I'm not available. There are plenty of ladies waiting inside. Go bother one of them." She turned away and he pulled her back.

"Callum get your hands off me this instant!" she demanded. I had been listening in and had seen enough.

"Hey! What is going on out here?" I demanded. "You better take your hands off her majesty this instant like she demanded of you." He let her wrist go and stormed off inside the party. "What was that about?" I questioned her still in anger. "Is he someone you care for?"

"No," she said as a tear fell, "I spent last summer with him. It has been almost forty years since I had seen you last. I'd been waiting so long and doubted you were ever coming back to me."

"I don't need to hear this, I don't need an explanation."

"I did wait for you. I was just so lonely."

"Irena stop," I spurt out! I did not sound like my usual self. She paused.

"I'm sorry. I feel awful about it," and she walked back inside looking shameful. I wasn't sure why what I had witnessed bothered me so much. I cared for her more than someone should care for a stranger that they had only just met. We sat together without speaking for the rest of the evening. She was queen, so she had to seem strong and stay late into the night until the last of her guests left because her absence would seem rude and improper. I could tell she was holding back the tears. When the party was over, Emeth came to escort the queen back to her room. Only a few people remained. She said goodnight to the rest of her guests and they thanked her for the magical evening. "The pleasure was mine," Irena would tell them. It seemed exhausting to have to always be so proper and entertain.

"May I speak to you for a moment?" Irena asked me before she left.

"Not here," I said and then Theo ran up to us.

"Wow, what a night!" "I think I fell in love." Emeth rolled his eyes at me and we all four of us walked together to our quarters.

"I have to speak with Alick a moment."

"If you wish my dear," Emeth agreed, not wanting to interfere. He watched me closely as I passed him going into her chambers. Emeth and Theo waited for us in the hall outside her door.

"I wanted to apologize for what you witnessed. I can't even begin to tell you how guilty I feel."

"You really don't have to apologize. I understand. I really don't see how anyone could wait that long for someone anyway."

"But I have waited. I messed up obviously spending my time with that fool. Deep down I always believed you would return no matter how hard it was to wait. I had to. It's all I had left; the hope that I might see you again."

"Listen, Queen Irena, even though I'm physically here, my mind is not the same. I don't remember you or have any of the same memories that you have of us together. I'm not that person anymore, if I ever was."

"You don't really believe that, do you? Don't say it. You don't mean it."

"You can be with whomever you wish. The Alick you knew is dead. He's gone. He isn't here anymore!" She was crying hysterically for me to stop.

"He's not gone; he's standing right in front of me." She tried to come close to hold me and to kiss me, but I was unsure. The poor girl needed to let it go. I wasn't allowing her to suffer any longer. She needed to let this Alick go. It was her weakness. I wasn't real. The image she had in her head wasn't real, only an old memory of someone else. She had her hands up grabbing me and fought me until we both fell to the floor. She finally gave up and started crying again. I felt bad for her. I watched her and listened to her cry. I couldn't take it. Now I felt bad for saying what I had said. I felt like it was now my duty to comfort her in some way, but wasn't sure how.

"Emeth said I may never get my memory back." She said nothing. I had broken her. I thought Emeth would have a better idea of what to do so I started walking over to the door and, just before I reached out to open it, I had a thought, 'What if there was even a slight chance she was right and somewhere deep within me is the person she once knew?' I would never know if I walked away and left her there alone with Emeth. What if she had wasted her whole life believing in something that didn't exist? I could at least help her find out for sure. I owed her that much. I decided to try, "Irena." She looked up at me. Her pitiful face was red and puffy from the tears. I looked down at her, unsure of what I was doing. I marched over to her, knelt down, and pulled her face to mine and kissed her with all that I had.

All of the lights around us started to flicker. The lights outside in the hallway where Emeth and Theo stood started flickering as well.

"What's happening?" asked Theo.

"He's remembering," Said Emeth. A spark of energy numbed my lips and traveled through my entire body. I opened my eyes, different for a moment as looked at her. I remembered seeing her standing on a beach somewhere. I tried to remember more but nothing else came to mind.

"Do you know me?" she asked desperately.

"I'm sorry. I still don't remember anything except that I have seen you once before, when you were slight younger, I think. We have met somewhere before, and that's all I know."

She smiled, "Yes and that's alright. At least we know your memory can come back. I knew you would try." I was still stunned at what had happened. Someone knocked at the door.

"You may enter," Irena called out. Emeth walked in.

"It's getting late," he said. I left her with Emeth, lost in thought and walked right past Theo without speaking. There was my proof. I had known her in a previous life although I could not remember from where, which frustrated me so. Everyone was right all along and I was wrong. The idea was ludicrous and I felt so foolish at having not believed anyone. The entire evening had spun me like a wheel and left me unhinged. I paced for hours in deep thought until I was emotionally drained and couldn't take in a single thought more for the night. Then I passed out into a deep sleep exhausted. That night I dreamed constantly of the girl that I had recognized standing on the shore. I knew her in my dreams. I felt like I had had the same dream a million times before. What did it mean? From the occurring dream that night, my mind couldn't decide whether to drift off further into sleep of peace from seeing the girl standing there, or to awake from a sudden nightmare from seeing her face again. As soon as I would awake from the nightmare I would dose back off into another deep sleep once more with the same reoccurring dream. In the morning Theo awoke me. From my restless night I hardly wanted to move.

"Get up," he started shouting as I failed to respond.

"I'm just going to lay here a little longer Theo," I replied.

"Oh no, that's not like you Alick. You always beat me up before sunrise. Come on!" I rolled over agitated. I was so tired my eye lids burned and I could barely keep them open. We ate our usual breakfast together. I kept yawning.

"I guess you didn't sleep very good last night," he noted.

"Really? I didn't notice," I said smartly.

"Grumpy," he added. I finished the rest of my meal in silence. Like brothers, we argued constantly.

12. To Meet A Dragon

The doors to the great hall opened abruptly and Emeth marched in quickly.

"Come now, we have a great beast spotted only about a mile from our borders." We both jumped up out of our seats and followed Emeth to our weapon chamber.

"What is it?" asked Theo.

"A village nearby was nearly half destroyed by what they are claiming to be a dragon."

"A dragon?" I asked again in disbelief.

Emeth responded, "No one has seen a dragon for decades. I have never seen one in all my years or even heard of one being spotted before. I have thought of them to be extinct. They usually kept in hiding in dark caves or had an underground lair." Emeth told us all that he knew of them from reading books, "The only reason I can imagine the dragon would have come so close to such a large city would be the river that's not too far away. There is a river that runs right beside the village where the people have sent word claiming the beast attacked. We need to send men to hunt the dragon down and kill it. It could come further into our land."

"Well that's easy," Theo said sarcastically.

"I'm sending both of you with several of our best men to track down the beast. If it comes to it and either of you are faced with any harm, retreat. Do not try to be heroes. We know nothing else of dragons except that they are very dangerous." Emeth handed us large swords, armory, and shields. "The people from the village are calling this particular dragon a great fire breather." We climbed on our horses, ready to ride off with the other prepared soldiers. Emeth ended his rant by saying, "Do not delay. Finish the mission and get back here. Both of you be careful." We were off across the field and straight into the forest. We quickly passed the guards holding down their post at the border. Before we knew it, we had arrived at the village. Some of the huts were completely destroyed and still had smoke rising from above them. There were a few distraught people coming up to us and explaining what had happened. A strange man came up to me and said, "Come with me. I'll take you to Old Ramus. He has been this before and will know what to do." Theo and I looked at one another and agreed to go with the odd stranger. I dropped down from my horse and followed the man to a round hut made out of straw where I found the older man named Ramus that the odd man had spoken of. Theo waited outside. He was sitting on colored blankets and had a fire in the middle of his tent. He was old and dirty and playing with different powders, throwing them into the fire and chanting an unheard language. I thought he was a lunatic. He had a white beard that grew almost to his waist. It was the longest beard I had ever seen. He looked up and saw me and the other man enter.

"Ah! Finally. Come in, come in." There wasn't much room in the small hut where he stood and offered for me to sit.

"Sit down, sit down," he murmured.

"Old Ramus, Can you help us?" I asked.

"You don't' need helping; you just need to regain your memory," he responded.

"How did you know about that?" I questioned him, startled.

He was staring into the fire like he was watching something play out. 'What an odd little man,' I thought to myself. He was holding a stick and started pacing back and forth, still mashing different items up and casting them into his fire.

"We are in a hurry. If there's something you know then please share it with me!" He ignored my comment.

"When I was younger, I lived in the mountains. There were three baby dragons abandoned in a cave which were found and raised by my grandfather. When I grew up, the dragons grew and became larger than I was, but were still considered babies. Over the years I have seen miraculous things. My grandfather rode a dragon once by accident. He fell off of his roof by mistake and the dragon saved him by breaking his fall before he hit the ground. But when I was older, the same dragon turned on my grandfather for no reason at all and ended up killing him. Just like any wild animal, you never know how they will respond. Dragons can never be tamed."

"Thank you for the information. It was very helpful," I said as I began to stand to leave.

"Wait just another moment," he kept shuffling through random jars. "There it is. Here." He handed me a handful of what looked like different colored stones.

"These are dragon scales. Keep these on you and the dragon can't smell your scent. Dragons choose who they let ride them. If you can somehow manage to get onto his back long enough to ride into the air, he will be your dragon." He then handed me a small satchel. "Here are some mice to help you train the dragon. Mice are like a treat to them."

"I thought you just said dragons could not be tamed?"

"They can't and few have ever dared, but you are different now, aren't you? You cannot control his behavior, but once you ride him, you will always be able to ride him. My grandfather was able to ride his for years. Just remember that you can never trust a dragon's spirit. They can turn on you." I thanked him for his help.

"Oh, one more thing," I turned and he blew some sort of powder in my face and also into the fire. A force field of glittery looking dust traveled outward from the fire.

"What are you playing at?"

"It was the last ingredient," he said.

"For what," I asked?

"To help bring back your memory faster. Remember to stay close to the queen," he ended. I walked out of the hut unsure of what had just happened. Theo came up in front of me on his horse.

"Did you just see that? Some sort of magic is here."

"I know. Let's go. I know what we have to do!" I jumped onto my horse and we rode off into the direction everyone from the village explained they had last seen the dragon. We headed into the woods to track the dragon. As we were walking I quietly told Theo everything the crazy old man had said to me.

"You can't ride a dragon," he told me. "We have to kill it so it doesn't do any more harm. That's what we were sent here to do."

I replied, "Listen, we're unsure if we can kill it. Instead of taking the chance of injuring our men and the dragon getting away, you all can distract him while I sneak up on him and jump on his back. I have these scales which will keep me invisible from his senses. Imagine what we could do having a dragon on our side in the battle against the dark army? If something goes wrong while I attempt to jump on him, shoot him with all your arrows."

"I don't like the idea," Theo said. "My grandfather told us to come back in one piece."

First we had to find the dragon and it was becoming late in the afternoon. We didn't want to be caught out here in the dark. Theo said he had heard dragons were mostly nocturnal, if that was true, we were more likely to be attacked at night than during the day and, just maybe, we thought, the dragon could possibly be sleeping whenever we came across it.

"What if something goes wrong? What if the old man was wrong about these scales and they are old and don't work anymore?" Theo asked still sounding worried. He continued, "Or say the dragon can't smell you. I'm sure he will still be able to hear you. What then?"

"I'm going to sneak up on him slowly. Just stick to the plan and trust me," I said trying to reassure him that everything would be alright.

"Well I guess I have no say in the matter?"

"Shh," I said covering Theo's mouth. All of the men behind us froze. I heard movement from over in some bushes and peeked through. The dragon was on the other side of the river having just gone swimming and was lying to dry down on the grass. Theo and I watched him attentively. The dragon was gigantic like we expected, I guessed around twenty feet long or so. He had yellowish and burgundy tinted scales with a purple tongue like a snake and two bent back horns on the top of his head. He looked like he was only resting for a moment. This was maybe our only chance. We knew we couldn't be noticed yet or he would have probably already attacked us. I looked back at our soldiers.

"Don't move," I said quietly. "If you need to shoot the dragon, will your arrows be able to reach from this distance?" I wanted to confirm my plan was sufficient.

"Oh yeah, plus a couple more feet. I've got this from here." Theo replied confidently.

"Alright then I'm up. Don't miss."

I vanished through the brush. I knew my part must be done quickly before the dragon decided to move or we could be spotted. I sprinted fast up the riverside because I had to cross without being seen. I made it across the river without being noticed. The dragon was turned the opposite way. Now was the tricky part. I had to move slower as I came closer to the dragon so I wouldn't be heard as I snuck up on him. As I came closer, his size seemed to increase. This was the creature of everyone's fears. I started to re-think my plan. I really hoped my plan would work without failure and I had made the right decision. The scales must have worked; the dragon hadn't stired at all. I started climbing the nearest tree. I looked across the river and could see Theo's face looking through the brush back at me, ready for anything that could happen. The horses must have made some sort of noise because the dragon suddenly looked up in Theo's direction.

Now was my chance. Ready or not, I had to take what could be the only opportunity. I let go of the branch and jumped down onto the dragons back, avoiding his wings. The dragon, not expecting me, let out a growl and breath of fire, which was so loud I couldn't hear for a few seconds after. Theo and the others jumped out from behind the bushes, yelling for the dragon's attention so it wouldn't focus entirely on me. The dragon started to lift his powerful wings up off of the ground to get away. He looked shiny and slippery and I was expecting it to be harder to hold on to him and thought, maybe, I would fall off easily. However, he was rough and jagged and I had a good grip. I pierced his skin around the top of his neck with an arrow so I would have something easier to hold onto and he let out another roar. I was unsure of how far up a dragon flew and was trying not to fall off. We were out of the trees. I looked down at Theo and the others who had their swords and shields lifted and arrows pointed, ready for attack. The dragon breathed out one more breath of fire at them, which reached to my surprise. They all ducked and covered themselves with their shields. They looked fine as I leapt into the air. We were off. The others looked like little specs from the height I had reached now. I held on with all of my strength. I dropped a rope down over the dragons shoulder hoping to be able to wrap it around his neck, making it easier to hold on. It was no use at the moment. The dragon kept getting higher up and the rope flew back at me. I had to wait. I was so concentrated on what the dragon may do next that I hadn't noticed we were above the clouds. We kept rising, higher and higher. It was very hard to breathe the air this far up. The air was very thick. Luckily, the dragon could barely breathe either because he started to drop again. He stopped in midair for a moment. I quickly threw down the rope again and reached to grab it from the other side of his neck. As soon as I grabbed it he jolted straight down. I was holding onto both ends of the rope tied around the dragon's neck. Since I had to lean in closer to grab it, my legs were not dug into him any longer for my grip. As the dragon dove it felt like falling. My feet were straight up in the air, but I held on. I wasn't about to let go of this rope, even if I was upside down. This was my dragon. My life depended on it. I held on with all that I had as we came closer and closer to the ground. For a moment I thought the dragon was about to give up and fall to his on death, but, at the last minute, he lifted up again. We started inclining slowly. He was giving me the ride of my life and not making the capture easy for me.

The rope was tied now in a knot and we rode off into sunset. The dragon was living up to his name and didn't want to disappoint. We flew faster and he started turning back and forth trying to shake me off. He then started doing swirls through the clouds and a few times I almost fell off when we were upside down. After a while I could tell the dragon was tiring out and began flying at a steadier pace. Finally, I thought I was in the clear. I held on tight in case he should try to take off again. The sun set and I rode him for several more hours into the night. The breeze at night was peaceful from up here and the view was amazing. I was flying. I started rubbing him and speaking to him to establish trust if that were possible. The dragon needed to get used to the sound of my voice. He looked back at me as we were flying. He had finally calmed down. I started pulling the rope, guiding him in the direction I wanted to go. At first he was stubborn, but after a while he gave in and listened to what I was telling him to do. I aimed him towards the ground and the moment of truth. What would happen after we landed? Would the dragon still try to kill me? We flew down into the dark pastures and green hills. Nothing but the bright moon was shining for light. The dragon's eyes reflected the moon and glowed bright yellow. We landed. He gave off another protective roar as a warning. I wanted him to know I wasn't going to try anything. My plan was to distract the dragon with raw meat so I took out a dead mouse I had kept in my pocket from Old Ramus. I held it out as I climbed down. My shield was ready in case he wanted to try anything. He stared at the field mouse and followed it with his eyes. I threw it into the air and he caught it with his mouth. I took out another one and fed him again.

"Good dragon," I said. "What shall I call you?" What sounded like a dragon name? "How about Samsun," I suggested and he roared. "Alright, hmm, how about Mecarth?" Not a sound. "Okay, Mecarth it is," I said as if he had agreed. The old man was right; there was no way to predict a dragon. They had strong temperaments, but, with a little training, maybe they could be taught. Even though I didn't know for sure, I felt like Mecarth respected me for riding him. No human has ever dared to try to freely ride a wild dragon before and I stayed to live to tell the tale. Now I just had to manage a ride back home. But it had to count for something.

I fed Mecarth my last field mouse and hoped this time he would let me climb back on his back. I kept thinking he may fly off and I would never see him again. It took me almost an hour to get close enough to touch him again. I pet his side. I didn't want to try and climb on him right away and spook him. Finally, I crawled upon his back and we were off in the air again; this time I was in full control. I was confident after I rode him that he considered me his master and I now felt a deep connection with him that I couldn't explain. This time the ride was more enjoyable. The scenery was amazing and breeze high in the night's sky. Mecarth wasn't trying to throw me off this time and flew in a straight line at a steady pace. My next step in training him was to teach him my sounds of command so he would know when I called. I whistled as we rode so he would know the noise well and be used to it. I wasn't sure a dragon should be kept near the city. Mecarth was a free animal and would resist staying put for long. If we kept food near the city for him, he would not have to go far to hunt for himself. The castle was built on a huge hill, so maybe we could build the dragon a cave on the other side away of the city. I did not want the people to be alarmed with a dragon living nearby.

I had all of these ideas filling my mind on the way back, riding Mecarth. I hadn't even noticed we were almost there; time literally flew. The city lights were gorgeous from up here. As we came closer to the ground, I could see many soldiers from down below waiting on us, watching us. Mecarth roared and for a moment I worried they would make a mistake and try to shoot the dragon, not seeing me on his back. We were high up and it was dark. I kept my distance and we finally landed safely about fifty feet away from the crowd of people. I slid off Mecarth and stood in front of him at a safe distance. I continued whistling for his comfort and reassurance. I looked back at the line of soldiers.

"It's alright," I calmly said, "he isn't going to hurt anyone."

Emeth stood in front of the other men, "Alick, is it safe for me to approach?" he asked.

"Just you and do it slowly," I said. Some of the men had netted ropes ready to tie up the dragon. When Mecarth saw them he became uneasy. "There there, it's alright," I tried to reassure the creature and turned to Emeth who had paused on his way over. "Tell them to lower their weapons." Emeth signaled them to do so and then continued walking over to me. Mecarth started grunting and growling as Emeth came closer to us. When he was about ten feet away, I said, "That's close enough Emeth and don't make any sudden movements."

"Theo explained to me when he returned what you had done. I told you we needed to kill the beast," Emeth said and Mecarth roared once more. "Theo said the dragon took you up in the sky and above the clouds until he could no longer see you. Theo left out to search for you and still hasn't returned."

"Here I am," I said.

"You could have been killed Alick. What were you thinking?"

"Well I'm very much alive," I replied

We spent the next half hour conversing about what we could do with the dragon. Emeth asked questions like, "Where would we keep it?" I told him all of the plans I had for Mecarth and that I would be the only one to go near him to feed him.

"He's dangerous, not a pet," he argued.

"No, he isn't a pet. He's a weapon and now my responsibility," I added, "A weapon that we very much need," I added.

"Very well," he finally gave in, "I do not think it is a wise decision to keep this dragon around our people, but I will trust your judgment, since you are the only one who truly knows the dragon." I thanked him. After Emeth's blessing, I now needed to speak with Agrius right away. However, I could not leave Mecarth's side on the chance he would fly away. Agrius would look too much like food to Mecarth. I wished Theo was here to be the messenger. Emeth would have to do, although he would over analyze everything.

"What happens now?" Emeth asked.

"Ok listen, first I need you to go and tell Agrius to gather as many men as possible to help him dig a hole on the other side of the mountain. One that is large enough to be Mecarth's cave, where he can feel safe and content. Tell him to lead the strongest men tonight to get it started; I really need this done by noon tomorrow."

"Noon tomorrow? It is tomorrow." Emeth replied.

"Well then we don't have much time. Let them get started then. I can't leave Mecarth's side until I know for sure he's comfortable enough to be left alone or he may fly away and all I have done would have been for a waste." Before Emeth left I also told him to find a farmer that we could buy some goats from so we could keep Mecarth well fed. I wasn't sure of a dragon's appetite or how long the field mice would last before he became hungry again but I didn't want to catch him at that moment. Emeth looked weak from being up all night and as he left I told him to get some rest. I looked over across the field at Agrius as Emeth told him my plans. Agrius nodded to me from across the lawn and quickly left with several men that were standing around him.

As the first sign of daylight started to break through the trees, I climbed onto Mecarth's back once more and rode away from all of the people and the city. It was safer this way in case Mecarth was tempted to attack someone. By lunch time Mecarth's new home should be built and I would head over with him. Until then we rode through morning. I wanted him worn out and ready for sleep when we made it to his new cave. He also needed to be full. After flying a while, I spotted a deer in the forest down below.

"Come on Mecarth," We dropped down out of the sky. "That's it. Let's see what you can do!" I could steer him in any direction, but it was up to him; he was in control of the rest. His claws came up and pierced the deer and then lifted the body up off the ground. The deer never saw Mecarth coming. 'Outstanding' I thought. The dragon landed and I jumped off and backed away as he ate. He ate aggressively and I didn't want him to mistake me for his food or to think I wanted the deer for myself. I sat there the rest of the morning watching him, trying to learn his tendencies. Dragons were unpredictable. The dragon was the most intelligent animal of all; I was sure of it. When I rode him, it was almost like he knew exactly what I wanted him to do; like he somehow knew my thoughts. I could tell he was ready to sleep. "Come on Mecarth, we're almost there." I hoped the cave would be ready for him.

Just then I noticed soldiers from the dark army camping from down below. Until now no one had seen them travel this close to our city before. We knew the days for war were getting closer and closer.

This was only further evidence. For a second I thought about taking Mecarth down for a spin, but Mecarth was too valuable to me and I knew he was tired. I wouldn't worry over a few soldiers just yet. I knew where they were and could send some of our men to return and kill them. Just then, I saw a quarrel between some of the soldiers over something and decided to circle and watch to see what they were up to. That's when I noticed that they had captured Theo. He was on his knees and looked like he was begging for his life. There was no time to send men back to rescue him. I had to save him now if I wanted him to live. I had no strategic plan, but I knew I had to act fast. The dragons shadow went over them as they looked up to the sky to see what it was. They all became quiet and listened. Mecarth and I came out of the trees and he blew fire all around them. Some fled, but most stood their ground. I jumped off to fight back.

"It's a dragon; Shoot it!" One commander started shouting orders. I came up from behind him and killed him quickly with my blade. Some men started shooting arrows at Mecarth, but kept missing because he was too fast. I grabbed Theo from off the ground. He had a puffy face from having been beaten and I could tell that his body was sore. I helped him get away from the burning tents and into the trees to hide.

"Stay here," I told, "I'll be right back." I had to make sure Mecarth was alright. I took down a few more soldiers by surprise and then I saw Mecarth get shot in the wing by an arrow. He let out another roar and burst of fire and then flew off. 'Damnit,' I thought. I wasn't sure if he was coming back for me or how Theo and I were going to escape now. I heard a foot step from behind me and turned. Another soldier had Theo with a sword to his neck. I raised my sword.

"I'll kill him if you take another step," the soldier said. "Lay down your sword."

"Don't do it Alick," Theo shouted!
I started putting my sword down slowly, unsure of what else I could do and suddenly, out from nowhere, Mecarth appeared and as he screamed in terror, Mecarth bit down on him. He swallowed the soldier whole. Theo fell to the ground in pain and I ran over to him. I lifted him on top of Mecarth and we rode off quickly in case any other soldiers were still alive to come after us.

"What happened back there Theo?" I questioned, "How in the world did *you* get captured?" Theo was still quiet. "Answer me," I demanded.

"I deserve to be dead," he kept saying. We landed in a field that was open and safe.

"What do you mean?" I asked.

"I betrayed everyone Alick, even you."

"What are you talking about," I asked again.

"Growing up my father was hard to impress. He wanted me to be great at everything and I wasn't good at anything."

"You're the best bowman I have ever seen," I said, confused, "I'm sure you practiced a lot."

"I did and never improved. I wish you could have seen the disappointment in my father's face. One day, when I was about to turn eight, I was playing alone. I had no friends," This didn't sound like the Theo I had known. "I came across the ancient portals and sat down beside one to rest and think to myself. A man appeared and spoke to me through the portal."

"A man?" I questioned.

Theo nodded his head and continued, "He promised me that if I brought him information that he asked of me, he would bless me with the talent I had always desired."

In shock I asked, "Theo, what are you saying?" I couldn't believe it, not Theo.

"For that whole next summer I did what he asked of me. I told him things like what the princess had been doing, how many soldiers we had, some of our battle strategies and, in return, I became the best archer anyone had ever seen before. My aim improved instantly from not even hitting a target to on point each time. I suddenly became the talk of the town and had more friends than anyone could ever ask for. I enjoyed every minute of it, particularly the new change in my father's eyes and attitude when he looked at me. He was proud." Theo suddenly had tears in his eyes. "The next summer our village was attacked. I watched my mother and father as they were killed by the same man I had been helping through the portals. Princess Irena used her powers to save who she could, but it was too late for my parents. This was before the castle was built and our city grew into thousands.

That's when she put up the protective wall with her powers. The portals did not work after that. I know because I went back to them to try and kill that man but he never appeared again. For years I blamed myself for my parents' death. I didn't know it was Damion that I was helping, but I still knew it was wrong. I led him to us, and that's how he killed my family and that's how he knows where we are now. He's been preparing for us for years and he's not that far away. We only have a couple more weeks at best. I thought by not giving him any more information, my talents would disappear, but then I realized it wasn't the information I had traded with him, it was my parent's lives and my soul. I traded my soul." I shook my head, not knowing what to say. I remembered how, once upon a time, Theo listened to my story and tried hard to understand.

"Theo you were only a child; you didn't know what you were doing. Damion has a way of getting under everyone's skin and tricking us. His promises are lies. You are a good archer because you believed in yourself. Your talents haven't gone away because they are your own."

"I am haunted every day," he said.

"If there's any advice I can give you, it's that the past is over and there's nothing you can do to change it. You have learned the lessons you were meant to learn through your mistakes and as long as you have learned what you were meant to learn then there is no such thing as failure."

I helped him to his feet, making sure nothing was broken. His arm was dislocated and I had to push on his shoulder to put it back into place. Other than that, he was only bruised and looked like hell. I sat with him the next few hours, talking with him, and he seemed to calm down. He admitted to me that the reason he gave me a chance when I told him my story about the dark army was because, in a way, he had also helped them once before himself. We finally flew back after I promised to keep everything I had learned to myself. He said he wanted to tell Emeth when he was ready. I ended our conversation by telling him that there would never be a *right* time, but that he would finally feel free by telling the truth. We landed after dark at the entrance of the manmade cave. Several men were still finishing up and waiting on us there.

"Good Lord Theo, what happened to you?" One of the men said.

"Get some rest Theo," I said as a servant wrapped a blanket around him and escorted him back to the castle. I looked up at Mecarth, "It's just you and me," I said, "let me look at that arrow." I could tell he was complaining in his own language. It would be tricky getting it out of his wing without hurting him any further. Luckily he was able to fly us back home. I knew he was having a hard time. I broke the arrow in half as it was still pierced through his wing and pulled the rest of it out. For a minute I thought he was going to bite my head off. "There it's alright. It's out." I poured water over it and gave him some fresh field mice as treats. "Good job today Mecarth. Thanks for saving our lives." We walked deeper into the cave. There was a goat tied up waiting on him inside where he was to sleep. "Go ahead. I will be back to visit in the morning," I said. I walked out myself tired, I hadn't slept the night before and was running on two full days with no sleep. I needed to crash and debated sleeping here with MeCarth. When I finally made it back to the castle, I was swarmed with many people who had questions about Mecarth. Was he dangerous? How did I manage to ride him? Where was the dragon now?

"Everyone, please, it's late. I'll be happy to answer all your questions tomorrow after I get some sleep. I can assure you all that Mecarth is not dangerous, however, no one should go looking near him."
I walked off towards my quarters.

"Who the heck is Mecarth?" I heard them question each other as I walked away. I sighed as I turned the corner and there was Queen Irena waiting on me with her own questions. I hadn't spoken with her in a while. I shook my head.

"Alright let me tell you all about it. I can't say no to you. I won't promise I can keep my eyes open though." I was sure she would be judgmental like Emeth and have a few choice words for me.

"You can go get some rest and tell me all about it after you've rested. I just had hoped that you would share these sorts of things with me," she said.

"Irena I can promise you this: you are the only person that I have thought of the past few days and I want to tell you all about it."

She smiled, "Well, then, I expect a report first thing in the morning."

"Yes ma'am," I agreed.

She kissed me gently on the cheek and walked away. She turned at the doorway, "You know I was worried sick about you. Do you have any idea the rumors that were spreading around the castle grounds about you and that dragon?"

"Don't worry," I said, "I have no plans on dying a third time." I smiled and she smiled back.

"Goodnight Alick," she said and then disappeared into her library. I longed to speak to her and explain what had happened over the past couple of days. I needed to tell someone what I had experienced and learned along the way and I was sure she was the best person for me to confide in, but I was too tired. Finally, I made it to my bed chambers. I heard a noise coming from the bathroom.

"Theo? You in here?" No reply. Someone was in here with me. I drew my sword, unsure who it could be. To my surprise, Lady Jezebel popped out from around the corner of the bathroom entrance. She was just as startled as I was since I had my sword drawn.

"I'm sorry my lady. I wasn't sure who was in here. I didn't mean to startle you. What are you doing in my bed chambers may I ask?"

"Well, I was worried about you, you know? Playing with dragons and all, you are so brave," She responded flirtatiously as she began moving closer to me.

"Well thanks, but here I am, just fine and dandy, all in one piece." I said back.

"Yes, I like to make sure you stay all in one handsome piece."

"Umm, listen Lady Jezebel. I need to get some rest now. I think you should go."

"I was only checking on you Alick. You desperately need a bath. At least let me draw you some water before I go." She bent down at the tub and grabbed a rag.

"It's not that I'm not flattered, I just can't," I said.

"Oh' come on. Give in just a little bit," she said in a playful voice. It's only innocent fun. I promise. I think you deserve it."

Just then there was a knock at the door.

"Wait here." It was Theo at the door.

"Alick let me in," he said.

"Now isn't a good time," I replied. "You have to leave now," I told Lady Jezebel. I handed her a towel and pushed her out the main door.

"Wait a minute; you can't just kick me out."

"Goodnight Lady Jezebel." I slammed the door in her face and locked it shut. Theo was now banging on the door. "Coming," I said. I let him in. He still looked really bad. His face was swollen tight and bruised badly with one eye shut. "What are you doing out of bed?" I asked him.

"Rescuing you from making a horrible mistake," he said looking down at the lit candlesticks. "I heard her voice from the other side of the door. I know you and the queen are going through something right now, but I can tell it's coming back together again, and here you are going to mess everything up all over again." I didn't know what to say.

"Well, I wasn't expecting her to be here. How was I to know?"

"Women like Lady Jezebel are beautiful on the outside, but trouble, okay? You're just going to have to trust me on this." Theo said in return. "I'm not saying you were about to do anything. I was just looking out for you, making sure you didn't."

"Well I was about to send her out, but thank you Theo, you are right."

"Everyone makes mistakes. Trust me I know," he said as he walked back into his room.

I threw him a cold rag, "for your face," I laughed.

"Ha ha very funny," he ended laughed. "You best figure out how Lady Jezebel wound up in your room and make sure it doesn't happen again."

"Agreed," I said as I shut the door behind him.

I knew I had to make sure no one could sneak in my room so easily for Irena's sake and for my own reputation. "*Ah* finally," I thought, when I hit the sheets it was the best night's sleep I had had for a long while. In the morning I awoke bright and early and felt rested. I found out that the servant maids had shown Lady Jezebel into my room the night before because they were paid off. Theo decided to stay in the bed for the entire day. I was on my way down to speak with the Loriners who made harnesses for the horses and the Cordwainers who made fine leather to see if they could team up to make something special and one of a kind for Mecarth, something that had never been done before. After much planning they drew what I had asked of them and said it could be done. "Wonderful! How soon?" I asked. They looked at each other. The Corwainer, Mister Aker, said he would trim all of the leather parts needed down to the correct size and provide it by that very afternoon to the Loriners who were putting the rest together. I paid them each ten gold shillings for getting it done so quickly. "The sooner the better," I said. They both looked pleased and promised it would be done by the next day. After I visited and fed Mecarth and made sure he was doing fine by himself, I went back to the castle to check on Theo and speak to Queen Irena as I had promised her. I was running a little behind from all of my errands and didn't want to be any later than I already was. Several nobles were discussing important matters in the grand hall and ballroom. Some of the ladies in waiting were reading and studying in the library, which usually meant whispering quietly of the latest gossip, mostly about Mecarth these days. Normally I was interrupted by someone of importance when walking through all of these popular spots of the castle, but today was quiet and casual. By now most everyone had learned my ways. They knew I was usually in a hurry and very busy with something; most finally learned not to interrupt me with questions every time I was seen since I hardly ever answered the questions anyway. People waited for functions or royal gatherings to ask because I was usually happy to answer any concerns given to my attention at the right time. However, on my way back to check on Theo, Lady Jezebel stopped me in my tracks.

"We didn't get to finish what we started last night," she said. "Why don't I come by again tonight?" I told her as clearly as I could that nothing was ever going to happen between us. She dropped her head down and walked away, embarrassed, to some of her nearby friends, who were questioning her, and looking confused as to what I had just said to her. Some were staring at me and others in another direction. I turned to see Queen Irena was standing behind me. She was watching me as well and I hadn't noticed. I wondered how long she had been standing there. She hurried off in another direction and I quickly followed behind her. As she went down a narrow hallway that lead into some other smaller rooms of the castle, I called out for her to wait. We went through several passageways and people left as we walked through, respectfully, giving us some privacy. She did not slow down and, when I finally caught up to her, I regretted it. Years of built up frustrations poured out of her. It had nothing to do with Lady Jezebel, although I'm sure that's what set it off. She said on her way back to her room last night that she had seen Lady Jezebel coming from my bed chambers. After that start of the conversation, everything after took a turn for the worse. Theo might have been wrong about our relationship mending back together; it did not seem to be headed into better days. Irena couldn't take another day being with someone who wasn't really here for her. Her hope for me had run dry. She admitted that she had been lonely for years, and had looked to someone else to fill the gaps. When it did not work out, she accepted being alone until her time had come to an end. Now that I was here, it was just a reminder of all of her pain, and she couldn't share her feelings with me still.

"Why Irena?" I asked.

"Because Emeth was right. You won't ever get your memory back, and, even if you do," She became quiet.

"What?" I tried to get it out of her.

"It will be too late," she said.

"What are you saying?" I asked, not sure what she had meant.

"I may only have a couple weeks left at best, Alick. I'm going to die."

"No you're not. I'm going to make sure of it."

"It's ok I've accepted it. I've lived a longer life than most, and now I have accepted that we are over. Nothing will ever be the same between us." The words stuck and hurt. I wasn't sure how this was all going to play out. I'd had mixed feelings the entire time. I couldn't blame her. Finally, someone had spoken the truth aloud.

"How could it ever be the same if you don't even remember who I am?" she added.

"So that's it then. Yeah," I said hoping she would disagree with me like she usually did. She just nodded and walked away only because I was sure she couldn't say the words out loud and there I was, left alone with nothing else to say. Sure that whatever had been between us had ended forever.

13. Final Days

I knocked on Theo's door. "Come in," He said.

"Hey, are you doing alright?" I asked him.

"Oh yeah, never better," he said sarcastically. His face was still puffy, but the swelling had gone down some.

"You look a little better. I was just checking on you." I said.

"What's the matter with you?" he asked. It was amazing how he could tell something was wrong with me by just the tone of my voice. I wasn't sure if I should keep telling Theo every single time something new happened between Irena and me. I thought it might be best to start keeping my business to myself.

"Nothing. I'll just be in my room for a while."

"I'd give anything to get out of mine," he said and I left him there with his nurse.

Later in the day I went out to get supper to bring back for Theo and me. If I didn't feel somewhat responsible for Theo, I probably would have just stayed in my room for the rest of the night. I ran into Emeth on the way down. He said he would like to speak to me. I followed him to his private study and he sat down in his usual spot.

"There's something in particular I wish to say to you," he said. "I just wanted you to know that this is the very reason I warned you to stay away from Irena. She was strong and confident before you came here. I didn't want her to get side tracked or worried about you and she has since you first showed up here. She needs to concentrate on only one thing, and that is to be prepared enough for the enemy she is about to face. I'm afraid for her now because she has lost her focus, which is why I feel it is best if you would keep your distance from her from now on."

"I don't think she wants to see me anymore," I admitted to him.

"If I really thought that were true, I wouldn't be telling you this now. Honestly I do not think you completely understand everything she has been through. She lost you twice as you know; you can't possibly know the damage that has done on her, not to mention all of the others she has watched die trying to protect her."

"I can imagine," I said, not happy with my word choice. Imagining was the problem; I needed to be remembering. So from what Emeth had told me, there was a chance that Irena still wanted me.

"If you care for her wellbeing at all, stay away from her, please. I am begging you as an advisor and as your friend. She doesn't need any more emotional damage."' 'That's what I was?' I thought. Maybe I should just leave? For the next couple of hours I had a raging battle of thoughts going back and forth through my mind. Should I go? Should I stay? I wanted to help however I could, whatever my role was. I wanted to stay and fight, and make sure Irena stayed safe. What if this was her destiny and I only held her back from it? I swear my emotions were torn just as hers were too. She had to defeat Damion. What if I was the reason she was killed, because she became distracted? And then I remembered what old man Ramus said. He had reminded me to stay close to the Queen. There had to be a reason behind it.

Through the night, I put together all the reasons why I should leave. It seemed to be a repeating circle of thoughts. What should I do now? I came to a point where I couldn't stand hearing my own thoughts anymore. After all the negatives I started to think of the positives. It didn't take very long after thinking of all the good to know what I needed to do. I made my final decision, and stood up to leave my room. I wasn't sure what time of night it was, but I knew it was late. No one was out except a few servants on their duties. I knew what I had to do. Something was calling me to do it, and I just didn't know how I was going to manage working it all out. I had made up in my mind that I would try one more time, and if Irena still didn't want to see me, then I would leave the city. But, if I could somehow convince her otherwise that this was right, I would stay for her. I would be there for her, whatever she asked of me, whatever she needed. This next outcome would determine my next move. There were guards outside her door. Although Emeth had warned me, I was somehow going into that room. I knew the guards had probably been told to keep me away from her and would report to Emeth first thing if I turned up. If Irena really didn't want to see me, I wouldn't have long to change her mind.

So I had to find a new way to get in without anyone knowing noticing. There were guards keeping watch all around her balcony from the outside. I dressed up as one of the guards and told one of them that I was there to relieve his shift. Surprisingly, he was easily convinced. That was way too easy, but to make sure he wasn't on his way to warn Emeth about me, I might have knocked him out and tied him up in a nearby closet just to be safe. After I went back to my post I counted the seconds I had between the times the other guards paced from one side of the wall to the other. They walked on a walkway lined with several columns. They both met at the same time in front of her balcony where I was standing and turned to repeat it again. The pace they were walking stayed the same. I had about forty five seconds altogether to climb her balcony without one of them seeing. I had to start as soon as they both reached the opposite sides so the columns would block their view. This had to be quick and, if I was spotted, I could be mistaken for an enemy. So I waited for my chance and counted to myself. As soon as they went behind the wall again I shot an arrow I had hidden in my armory up to her balcony until it caught. I pulled the rope to make sure it would hold my weight. I went up quickly and, as I came higher, I could see the soldiers from down below turning to make their way back. I was a little over half way there and hanging in the wide open for about ten seconds. I then reached the bottom of the balcony and my body was soon hidden from the guards. Almost there. Surely none of them saw me or I would have heard them call or start shooting at me. I lost my grip on the rope and slid two feet down, my feet dangling under the balcony. I lifted up my feet once more; the guard was nearly underneath me. Too close. I finally reached the top and pulled myself over the balcony just before he looked up. There was light coming from inside and fabrics hung to give her privacy for when she was outside on her balcony. Looking down I could see the entire city from the high view. I looked over the railing and it seemed that the guards gave no thought or effort to my missing status. Irena was up. I could make out her body image through the sheets of fabric hanging in the entrance. She was sitting in front of a mirror, brushing her hair.

"Who's there?" she said surprised as she stood up in a discontent way.

"Shh, it's just me Irena. Don't call for the guards," I said as I poked my head around the curtains.

"What are you up to Alick?" She asked as she wrapped a blanket over her silk nightgown.

"Irena, we have to do something about the night watch out there. If an assassin wanted to get in here and harm you, it would be only too easy," I said.

"So what are you doing? Testing that theory out?" She was trying to give me a hard time. "How did you get past the guards?" she questioned me further.

"Oh, remind me to untie one of them after I leave here," I said teasingly.

"Alick, how could you?" she huffed with a cute mad face.

"I had to. I had to talk to you without anyone finding out."

"About what? I've already told you how I felt. This is for the best," she said again.

"Says who Irena? Emeth?" I asked.

"How dare you," she snapped.

"Listen, I know you trust in him and respect his opinion, and he's always guided your decisions. That is fine, but sometimes you have to ask yourself what it is *you* want." She did not say anything back. "He is wise and loyal to you. He is also old and thinks in his old set ways and for whatever his reasons, and he has his mind made up about us not being together." She began to explain the reason.

"I know, Irena. He's spoken to me several times about your safety and I get it. I know all about the things you have endured, but I can't begin to understand why it should be harder with me around. If anything, it should make things easier for you. I know we had a past together and I desperately wish I could remember being with you. I promise I'll keep trying." Irena said nothing so I kept going. "We have something. We have chemistry, and now all we need is time. Time for me to regain my memory. Timing is key; timing is everything for us." She continued to listen as I poured out my feelings to her.

"I'm not sure I can promise you time," she finally spoke, "I'm not sure I have much more."
I thought of our previous spat from earlier when I told her I thought it would be best if I left.

I then said, "The one thing that continues to repeat in my mind is the man who told me to get closer to you. He was trying to tell me something. How else could my memory come back, unless I went to the main source? I need more time with you to figure this all out. I have kept myself occupied trying to distract myself from thinking of you, but it doesn't help. Often I think of you, if I'm being truly honest with myself." She smiled.

"What are you proposing we do?" she asked.

"While I respect Emeth, and wouldn't want him worrying about you any more than he needs to, I can come to you whenever you're free and we can spend time together then. I know you have a busy schedule most days, but, whenever you need me, I will come. We can do whatever you wish; read, talk, sit or not say anything at all. I just want to be here with you." She looked at me and nodded her head in agreement. "I'm glad you were up," I said.

"I don't sleep much anymore. My powers give me endless energy and I'm stronger than I have ever been before." I told her that was wonderful. "I can feel him getting closer to us every single day that goes by. He's very strong also."

"Damion?"

"Yes."

"I won't let him hurt you," I promised.

She was quiet and then said, "Here, you can go through this passage way to get back out without anyone noticing." She pushed open a secret door beside her bed frame, made out of the same wallpaper that was all around her room. I would have never guessed the secret passageway existed.

"Where does this lead?"

"Into the main library out of a book shelf," she said.

"I wish I had known about this way earlier. This is how you've been getting though the castle without a fuss?" I asked her. I stood in the doorway and I looked at her a while before leaving. She had gorgeous eyes and I really longed for another kiss from her. I decided it was best not to push my luck. We were on good terms again.

"Same time tomorrow?" I asked.

"Knock twice," she said.

"Goodnight my sweet Irena."

Just before I shut the door she reminded me, "Don't forget to untie that guard." I winked at her.

"Oh yeah, thanks for reminding me. I almost forgot," teasing her.

The passageway led straight into the library, and it was dark. After freeing the guard with my face covered, I headed back into my room safely without anyone ever knowing I had been gone, even Theo thought I had been sleeping the entire night. The next morning I doubled the guards outside of Irena's balcony. I went to the market to pick up the finished piece of Mecarth's harness. It was even better than I had imagined. "Perfect," I said, thanking all of the men that had worked so hard to put it together. It was a one of a kind piece for a dragon. This would make it so much easier to ride Mecarth, especially in a battle. That day I tried it out on him and, after a good feel, he took to it well. I could guide him easier and ride him more comfortably. The carvings in the leather were outstanding. I was very pleased with the finished work. I loved seeing something that I had envisioned come to life.

Impatiently I waited for the day to come to an end so I could make my way back into Irena's room. Rather than trying to force me into remembering her because of how much she desperately wanted me back into her life, she gave up her own desires, and instead, tried to except me the way that I was. It's hard not to love someone like that. She was queen and could have anything she wanted. She could demand that I stay by her side or had guards follow me continuously watching my every move. She permitted my own free will. I convinced her that I wanted her and nothing else. If ever a woman deserved the very best from a man, it was Irena. It was hard to explain the way she made me feel over the next few days. Even though I could not remember her and had no memory of her, she was in my heart. I cared for her more than myself. She had somehow always been in my heart and I was done trying to figure out something that came so naturally. I gave in to her every need. There was an unexplained urge I had to protect her. I did not need an explanation; I only knew how I felt and it was enough. Now, she would have to command someone to force me away from her side. Our meetings were secret every night, but I kept up with her during the day. The sun had finally gone down and I took a quick bath and headed out. Theo asked me what my plans were for the evening and I told him I was going to check on Mecarth, a small lie. Few people were left in the grand hall finishing their supper when I snuck into the library once again. Only two people were left inside and I waited for them to leave before I went to the very back row and opened the shelf that lead to the passageway to Irena's chambers. When I walked to the end, I listened for any voices coming from the other side of the wall before I knocked. I gently tapped on the wall twice and Irena opened the door soon after.

That night we sat and talked for hours, laughing and drinking a sweet red wine. Irena told me stories of us from when we were children and how we met and some of the stories from the years that followed. She told of the time that we had spent together. I couldn't remember any part of the stories she told, but they intrigued me; they somehow felt real by listening to them. I could tell she left certain things out and only wanted me to hear the good memories she had. The only memory I had was when she was just a girl standing on the beach in front of me. I was sure it was the day we met from what she had explained to me. It was the only memory that I needed to know for my proof.

"Sometimes I wish I could forget some of my memories," she told me after she had finished telling stories.

"No, the memories you have, good or bad, make you the person you are today. You should never want to change that about you," I told her.

"I'm sure I must seem very different now. Thanks for putting up with me and not giving up on me and for sharing those stories with me. I enjoyed them," I said as I yawned.

"In some ways you are different and in other ways you are the same," Irena said. That made me feel ecstatic to hear that I was still the same person she once fell in love with. "It's getting late. Same time tomorrow?" she asked.

"Yes ma'am!" This time when I was leaving she leaned over and kissed me on the cheek.

"Thanks for this," she said.

"Goodnight," I said and she looked up at me. "You may be a queen now, but you'll always be my princess."

"Goodnight my sweet Alick."

14. The Portals

Over the next few nights the same conversations continued and we became very close. She was very familiar to me and something about sitting with her and talking was so peaceful to me and comfortable. I was sure she felt the same way. One night she said she had something she wanted to show me and I could tell she was second guessing herself about whether she should or not. I was happy she trusted me enough to share it. She began to explain how the portals work.

"Certain power, whether good or evil, can open them and they are located all over the world," she told me. "Emeth has been studying them ever since you disappeared through one the last time we saw you." She continued, "I can open them myself and one time, with Emeth's permission and several tests made first on others, I traveled back in time through one." I was amazed and asked her many questions about how they worked. Irena explained when you first stepped through you had to think about where you wanted to be.

"Where did you go?" I asked.

"I went back to the night we were alone in the cave, which is why I started crying that night. If you go back to the past you are in your old body. We found out that much. Once we learned how the portals worked, Emeth let me go through only that once and I chose that memory out of them all. It had been twenty years since I had last seen you and I missed you so I had to go back and see your face again. My memories had faded of you. I needed to see you again for the strength to keep going." I asked her why we couldn't somehow use the portals to our advantage. "There are certain things that are dangerous that we later learned about the portals." Irena explained to me that out of all ten people who helped test out the portals, only two came back out. One man volunteered to see his dead wife from the past and another man went back to see his old home before it burned to the ground years before. They both said they first thought of where they wanted to be and then they were there, and about five minutes later, when they wished to go back through the portal, it was in front of him again. We learned to get back you had to wish to be back in the present time. The others were stuck in their own minds somewhere along the way and never returned. We assumed it was because they wanted to stay in the past. Irena then explained that that was only one of the risks of using the portals. There was also the fact that if you changed anything from the past you could also change the future. "I closed them down for good a few years ago," Irena said, "Damion found us after traveling through them." Theo came across my mind for a second, but I didn't want to mention it since I promised him I wouldn't share his knowledge of the portals.

"Why did you decide to tell me about all of this?" I asked as I knew there had to be some sort of reasoning behind it.

"Damion knows where we are. I put up the wall to protect the people, but he is strong enough to break it now, and he's coming soon. I can sense him like he can sense me. There shouldn't be any harm in using the portal one last time. I have one last working portal left that I never shut down in case we needed to use it for any reason."

"Are you saying you want me to use it?"

"I've been in the portal once before and found my way back, so I know how it works. I want to send you back in time when we were all together. Maybe, instead of me telling you the stories, you could see for yourself in person. And, maybe, if you could see for yourself an old memory of your own, then you might remember something else."

"The only problem is that you said when you first go in through the portal you have to think of where you want to go. How would I be able to think of somewhere from my past that I cannot even remember?" Irena looked over at her large mirror hanging on the wall and walked over to it.

"Is that it?"

She nodded her head and said, "You can't go alone. That is why we will go together."

"Has that ever been done before?" She told me no. "It sounds too risky. What if we get stuck in a place and, for some reason, cannot come back?"

"Well then at least we will be there together, wherever it is. It isn't prophesized for any of this to happen."

"Well you said it yourself; certain things or decisions can change the future. If this was never prophesized then that probably means we shouldn't be doing it. All for what, to bring back my memory, which may or may not work? This is madness!" Irena said that she had given this a lot of thought and already made up her mind.

"Well thanks for giving me a say in the matter." I said, unhappy with how she was handling herself.

"I will open the portal and we will walk through together. Once inside, I need you to keep your mind blank; clear your thoughts and think of nothing. I will imagine where we need to be. When we arrive, try not to speak to anyone. If you are unsure of whom they are, for it could change things. No one should find out we are from the future because no one knows that it is possible yet. You will be in your old body. Once we come back through the portal again, anything that happened to Alick of the past in those few minutes we were there will be a black out, but he shouldn't notice." I asked her how long we would have inside and she told me about five to ten minutes at best.

"Have you given any thought as to which memory you are choosing to take us back to?"

"Yes I have," she said as she grabbed my hand.

"Let's do this then," I said unwillingly. She held out her hand in front of the mirror and it started turning clockwise in slow waves.

"Together," she said as we stepped into the portal hand in hand. Once inside I closed my eyes and thought of nothing, which was extremely hard for me to. I tried to keep my mind blank like she had asked me to do. I still felt her hand in mine and after a few seconds I heard noise. I opened my eyes and we were at a party, a grand feast of some sort like nothing I had ever seen before. I looked over and Irena was beside me except this time she was only a girl. I looked down and I was just a boy.

"We are children," I said to her.

"We don't have long Alick. I thought if I brought you back here to this night when we were acquainted, you could see Avalon as it once was, it might be able to help you." A few people were watching us.

"What are we supposed to do? People are staring."

"We just finished a dance together and you haven't been told about my powers, of Damion, or of your immortality yet. Your father is in his room waiting for you. My father will come to dance with me soon and I need you to be back on this dance floor before we get thrown back. 'My father,' I thought. Irena looked over across the room at a long table. She had tears falling from her eyes.

"What is it," I asked her?

"My parents. I've always wanted to see my mother and father just one more time."

"Go to them; I'll be fine," I said.

She pointed, "Go through those wide doors and up the staircase to the left. When you reach the top, your father's chambers are right down the hallway at the very last door. Meet me back down the steps in ten minutes. Don't be late. My powers are keeping this open and won't work in here for very long." Irena's father started making his way over to his daughter and I quickly left the room, watching as Irena sprang into her father's arms. I turned and made my way up the stairs.

I walked up the staircase and straight down to the end of the long hallway like she had said. The very last door was now in front of me; I wondered if I should knock. I pushed open the door and there was a familiar looking man sitting on the bed in front of me. 'My father,' I told myself. I had never met my father. Curiously I stared at him.

"Come in my boy," he said in a recognizable voice. "We have much to talk about," he said. I could tell he was a simple and gentle man. I sat down on a wooden stool in front of him. I wondered how he was going to explain to me all of the things I needed to know, and what advice he would try and give me. He told me how much he loved me and explained about my birthmark, which was also new news to me. I had never thought anything of it before. He said I had a warrior's soul and that I was very brave. About three minutes had already passed. I knew what Irena said. No one should find out about the future. I had to spare him the time and, without explaining what happens in the future, I needed him to tell me what I should do. I wanted him to know who I was and I wanted to know him. I had no memory of my parents.

"Listen," I interrupted making up my mind. "I only have about five minutes to speak to you, so I need you to trust me." He was quiet and listened. "I am your son from the future. I lost my memory and I do not remember you or anything from my past. Irena and I have found a way to come back here for only a moment in hopes of triggering something to help me regain my memory. She thought seeing you again would help me."

"How is this possible?" he said aloud. I told him I couldn't explain to him anything of the future and that just by telling him, it was a risk. If anything varied off course from what it should be than it could change things. His head was down. "Since you can't see me in the future and you have to come back here to see me then..." he paused in mid thought. "It is how I suspected it to be then and the war won't be in our favor?" I couldn't tell him that he would die tomorrow, but he guessed that much and I wouldn't dare tell him that I died in the future not only once, but twice. I knew it would be hard to explain these things to him, especially with only the short time I had left. The only reason that I told him who I was so he would be able to prepare the real Alick when he came to and so he could comfort me now, which was selfish, but I felt like I needed to tell him. I wasn't going to sit here listening to things that I already knew. He had a strong willed soul. Without thinking anything of himself he stood up and gave me a hug. Some of my memories jolted back. I remembered my father.

"I remember!" I couldn't remember him ever giving me a hug before. Maybe it was that he knew he would die or maybe he knew we had survived. I hugged him back. I realized I only had seconds left.

"Father, I have to go now. Make sure when I come back into this room, you tell me everything I need to know."

With tears falling he said, "I won't say a word about any of this to anyone. I know what I must do." I thanked him for everything he had ever done for me and for raising me to be the person I am today. After one more pat on the back and the exchange of 'I love you,' I left him there. The last thing he said to me before I left was that he was proud of me for protecting her.

"I promised I would."

Back down the stairs I bumped into someone. He was standing right in my face. "Cadman," I asked?

"What's wrong with you Alick? Watch where you're going!" he exclaimed. 'I missed you, too,' I thought. After a quick shove from him, I could see Irena standing in the background. I knew we were enemies at that time and I couldn't do anything out of the ordinary here. Irena and I ran to each other, the walls starting to shake.

"What's happening," I questioned.

"It's time to go. Grab my hand," she said. "Close your eyes and imagine home." We were both shot back onto her bed chamber floor from the mirror. I helped her up and then hugged her ecstatically.

"I saw my father and I can remember him!" I said to her happily. "You were right; it worked." She kissed me excitedly, which I wasn't expecting. I felt another shock between us.

"Do you remember me?" she asked, impatiently awaiting my answer. I didn't want to let her down, but I only had to look at her to see the disappointment in her face.

"You remember your father?" She asked me again. "What about your father?" I explained that I could remember him as a person, a great captain, giving men orders, and disciplining me as a child.

"I can't believe I got to see him again. What about your parents?" Her face lit up again.

"Oh, it was wonderful. I danced with my father like I did as a little girl, and sat with my mother and played with her hair. That night was one of my favorite memories of them. I loved going back and seeing them happy." I didn't dare tell her that I told my father that we were from the future.

"Cadman!" I shouted.

Irena looked over at me, "What about Cadman?" she asked.

"I saw him. He bumped into me and I remembered him. I wanted to hug him when I first saw him, but then remembered I couldn't." After a moment of Irena being quiet, it suddenly dawned on me why Cadman was not here with us now.

"Did he die of old age?" No reply. "What happened to him?" I asked again.

"He was killed a few years ago in our most recent attack, before I put the protective wall up. Theo is his son."

Everything hit me all at once about what Theo had told me about his parents and how he blamed himself. I knew Theo's father ever since I was a child. Theo was like a son to me.

"I can only remember bits and pieces from my childhood. I do not remember my second life yet. I can remember meeting you on the beach and now I can remember us as children, but that is all for now. Please explain what else happened?" Irena told me that Cadman was forty when I died for the second time and twenty years had passed until my return. She could only keep one person young and alive, which I thought was Emeth. But why would Emeth want to live and watch his son grow old and die? She tried to keep both of them younger and wore herself down, her powers weakened. So she kept Cadman young for several years while Emeth aged even more and, after his death, she went back to keeping Emeth alive. Emeth was a little piece of everyone that had ever meant something to her. If she lost Emeth, she would've lost everyone that was ever close to her. After Cadman died, her powers began to strengthen again. She was only meant to keep one person by her side.

"Emeth should be almost one hundred years old and I have kept him in his eighties," she said. "I can't lose him or you ever again," she said to me. "I would rather die than keep living without you. You haven't had to watch everyone you have ever known or cared for die."

"I'm so sorry Irena," I said and reached out to wipe away her tears. Just then the mirror started turning again.

"What's happening," I asked her?

"I don't know. I've only seen it do this when something was changed. The mirror shows what we changed while we were there, but we were careful and nothing should have changed." We watched the battle. We saw fallen men and my father captured and beaten, about to be killed.

"I can't watch this Irena," I said and turned my head. I heard him talking to someone so I turned back to listen. He was telling Damion no matter what he tried to do, he would never win against the city of Avalon and that he had seen the future and we live. The mirror went blank again.

"Oh no Alick! You told your father?"

"It was my father. I thought I could trust him," I argued back.

"Alick, he told Damion!"

"What does that mean?" I asked.

"Damion probably tried to find out how your father could see the future and that is why he started experimenting with the portals to begin with. We didn't even know that portals existed until Damion actually used one as a weapon."

"What are you saying Irena?"

"I'm saying that because you told your father who you were, that was the whole reason you disappeared for the second time. Damion sent you through a portal. It's your own fault. I told you not to say anything," she paced around blaming me.

"Alright Irena, let's not blame each other. I told you we didn't need to use the portal in the first place. It was never written about."

"What's done is done; we can't change it now," she said.

"Let's go back again and this time I won't say anything," I suggested.

"We can't. It only works in a certain place once, and I don't have enough energy to use it again so soon."

I huffed, "You mean using it took away some of your power? Irena, you will need every ounce of your power in about a week.

"I knew if I told you, you would never let it happen. Now you can remember a lot more than you could before."

"Was both of us seeing our parents again worth me being missed for twenty years?" I asked and Irena started balling.

"I thought you would remember me!" I tried comforting her by saying that our trip to the past probably wasn't the reason I disappeared, but she was already a mess. Irena cried for most of the night and I stayed up with her until we both fell asleep together.

Early the next morning I had to sneak out when Emeth started knocking. Theo wondered where I had been and, like always, I kept brushing him off. His face was almost healed.

"I'm going to train some new recruits, are you coming along?" he asked. "Now is the time. We must be are sharpest," he added. All I wanted to do was stay in my room for a while by myself and think, but knew I needed to get in better shape and there was plenty around to do. For a few hours I helped Theo train some new archers and I practiced my sword fighting. We had all the weapons sent out to be cleaned and sharpened. I took Mecarth plenty of food to prepare him. The days were numbered. We knew the dark army was getting closer. It was almost time for everything I had ever dreaded, time for Irena to face Damion. The thought was almost too hard for me to accept. I knew it was her destiny to face him alone, but I couldn't bare thinking of any harm coming to her, maybe even death. The day went on very quickly because I worked hard and kept myself distracted from the thought of war. I felt ashamed for my decisions yesterday and not listening to Irena in the first place. Maybe if I had done what she said we could've defeated Damion years ago on that ship and I would have never left her for so long. Now his powers had grown just as strong as hers and there was always a risk that we could lose in the end. I had to make sure that didn't happen. I had to make sure Irena lived.

That night Irena and I didn't speak much. We just enjoyed each other's presence and snuggled close together. We were both scared. The one thing Irena did tell me that was important to know was that she thought the portal should be closed for good. The portals had always caused some sort of harm no matter how much good they brought and were just too risky if they fell into the wrong hands.

"We're not meant to change anything. There are reasons everything happens the way it does, and we can't see what it brings," she would tell me. Late that night Irena had several bad dreams and woke up in a sweat. I shook her.

"What's the matter?" I asked her.

"I know where he is."

The next morning Irena and I rode off early to the place she had dreamed of. It was an old castle in ruins not far from ours.

"This is where the battle will be," she explained. "He will be here in three days' time." The scenery was a mixture of trees, rocks, and ivy.

"Let's draw this on a map so we can strategize with to our people."

She stopped me, "It won't look like the same place after he arrives. The ground soil will be turned to ash. It will be a dark place, and many bodies will perish here." I knew what she spoke of; I had seen the same images before. Everything green would burn and the only view that would stay the same would be the rocks we were stepping over.

When we returned to Irena's castle the entire city was in a panic. Mecarth was flying around above the castle towers. I whistled for him and he flew over to us. I slapped the rears of the horses so they ran off inside the gates. The last thing I wanted was Irena's prized horse being mistaken for food. As Mecarth landed I told Irena to back away slowly. Irena came closer.

"Why must you always do the opposite of what I say?" She held out her hand and a light glowed over Mecarth. He calmed down. Irena was able to touch him even though it was said a dragon could only have one master.

"What did you do to him?"

"I calmed him down and now you won't have to whistle for him anymore."

"Why is that?"

"I put some of my powers inside of him so that from now on, whenever you are around, he will always find you. The same way you always find me," she said with a smile. Next we had to calm down a few angry citizens who didn't like having a dragon flying over their homes.

After the chaos, it finally calmed back down. Now there was Emeth to answer to. He wondered where we had run off together and why we were all of a sudden smitten by one another again. We both explained to Emeth that the war would begin in three days' time and now wasn't the time to separate us. We needed a plan and, for the next few hours, we all studied the maps and strategized. We looked over the map I had drawn earlier of the landscape. Irena had had visions of the dark army coming in from the West. Our army would be waiting on them. We would have the advantage of cover from what was left of the castle on the battle grounds and, when the dark army reached us, we would surprise them with more soldiers coming in from every direction until we had them surrounded and caught in the middle without an escape route. They had more numbers in their army than we did, but we had faith and hope that our strategy could work.

Later that night, in Irena's room, I said, "I wish you could see a vision of the outcome."

She replied, "I can't choose what I see; it just comes to me naturally sometimes." Her powers could be endless. I believed her powers grew stronger over the years because of her knowledge. We only had two more nights together. Out of fear of the unknown we held each other tighter that night and exchanged a small kiss.

15. The Tower

The next day Irena began having more visions of war. She decided it was best to stay in her room for the day. Meanwhile people visited with their friends in case it was the last time they would see one another. Mecarth was fed until full for what would be the last time before battle so he would be strong. The horses were fed oats and vegetables. They would be groomed, saddled, and ready to ride out early the next day. The soldiers' prepared and sharpened their weapons. I was confident in our soldiers, who were all well trained and experienced. Theo and I had made sure of it over the past few months. I knew Irena would not be able to sleep that night. She would want to feast with friends and spend the last few hours with the ones whom she loved most dearly in the world, so I convinced her to rest and take an afternoon nap. She needed all of her strength. Something was still so peaceful about her, even when she was terrified within her heart. I would watch her like a hawk tomorrow and not let her out of my sight. I spent an hour with Theo during the day while Irena rested.

"The day has finally come," Theo said. "Out of everyone here, who do you think wants to kill Damion the most?"

I looked at him and said, "Theo, don't even think about it." He was sitting there, sharpening his knife. I knew that look. "This may be the last time we get to sit together and have one of our important conversations," I said to him.

"Ah, none of that mushy stuff!" he responded.

"Well because after supper tonight I'm going to visit Irena."

"What's new?" he asked. Haven't you been doing that every night for the past two weeks?" He laughed and teased as usual. Nothing got past him.

"Listen, you be careful out there tomorrow."

"You too!" he said.

"I've got your back," I assured him and then left him alone, pondering to himself.

Emeth and I had a moment late in the evening as well. He said he had some important information for me to hear. Apparently old man Ramus, who had befriended me earlier in the month and helped me with the dragon, had been sought for by Emeth's guards. Emeth thought that if the man knew important information about the dragon, he might be able to help him with some other problems. There were some things you just couldn't find the answers to by reading books. He explained that the guards found no one fitting the description I had described, and the local villagers claimed that he was not a familiar face. Hardly any locals knew anything of him. The rumor was that old man Ramus was some sort of wizard and had disappeared without being heard from again. Emeth searched for him for two weeks and then called it off when there was no news. Wizards often travel to various places. Emeth questioned me to see if there was anything else he had told me that I could remember. Emeth said if there was anything else, it was more than likely correct. After he told me this, I said, "He did say that to help my memory I should stay near Irena."

Emeth responded, "I know things haven't been the same between us since you're return," he said to me. "I just want you to know that I've always been cheering for you, whether you believe me or not." He patted me on the back and I thanked him. He finished with, "Good luck tomorrow."

While the city finished with all of their daily routines and preparations, we stayed busy planning, helping others wherever we could with training, comforting, and anything we could possibly do to keep people calm and feel confident about what tomorrow would bring. Around sunset the city became very quiet. Everyone went home and spent precious time with their families. The women and children, including boys under the age of eighteen, would stay home tomorrow on the chance that if we failed, the protective wall would stay up long enough for them to prepare an escape. Men over the age of eighteen were trained for battle years beforehand. Theo and I had tried our hardest to train the youngest of the men ourselves over the past several months together. We taught them the importance of fighting to protect the ones they loved and to never kill unless it was necessary. We hoped our lessons would count and be worth all of our hard work. One day I hoped, long after this war was over, these brave soldiers would be remembered for what they had done on this day. Lives would be lost and families shattered, but brave men would always be remembered and loved. Hopefully, this would be the last war we would have to face. We intended to finish off Damion for good. I was sick of fighting. Our people deserved to live in peace without fear of the future.

The last of our allies arrived to help protect Irena's legacy. Some were princes or kings from other lands, awaiting the chance to defeat Damion's army for good. Damion had taken over almost every kingdom. The whole world was involved in this Great War, and this battle would be remembered in history. Avalon alone had thousands of people living here and, with our many guests, we were a crammed city. There were even some visitors who were not royalty, but had to set up tents outside the castle walls. Irena's welcomed all travelers with her kindness. All of the royals had a grand feast with us that last night. The city streets outside were quiet, but, inside the great hall, we were celebrating. The queen wanted a peaceful scene to draw out the anxiety of war. It reminded her of the night before Avalon was taken over, filled with family and friends. This could be our last memory together and we wanted it to count. Irena's father had always believed in celebrating family before anything else. Everyone ate, danced, laughed, and enjoyed the entertainment Irena prepared for the evening. She also delivered the rest of her supply of food to the people in case they would need to leave if we were defeated. Emeth presented Irena with a beautiful crown at dinner. Her hair was braided and had grown very long over the last few months. When she gave her final speech she said she was glad her path had crossed with many of the guests whom she could now call friends. She said everyone in the room was considered her family and that she had personally enjoyed each person's company during their visit.

After she thanked all of her supporters, her attention went to her own people. She told them no matter what outcome tomorrow might bring, she was happy to have led the city while time permitted and was proud of what it had become. I watched the people of Avalon as she spoke. Their attention focused on her with admiration. Some who worried for tomorrow were in tears; others stood or clapped, cheering her on. I also focused all of my attention on the woman I had grown to love over the past summer. The thought of tomorrow made me uneasy. I wondered what Damion would have planned for us. 'We can't lose,' I kept telling myself, 'we just can't.' Everything in me was ready to protect Irena. How could I watch her fight a person who wanted her dead more than anything else in the world? I had to help her any way I possibly could. She had told me many times before it was something she had to do by herself. When the time came, I knew she had to face him without me, alone. I wasn't sure how I could let her go. Just thinking of it made me upset and I grabbed her hand underneath the table and held it tight. She looked up at me and smiled, so calmly. She was fearless. A day couldn't go by without me seeing that beautiful smile; I couldn't live without it. If anything did happen to Irena, I already knew I would hate myself for it, and maybe, blame myself forever. I would want to die because I could not bear it. Out of everyone in the world, she deserved life. She deserved a life without fear and war. She deserved someone who loved her and would always be by her side; a life in which she could live peacefully and happy; a life in which she could celebrate family and love them every single day, not having to think of anything else.

Late in the evening the party abruptly ended. People made their way out the doors. Some wouldn't sleep at all that night. I prayed for a good night's rest for anyone who did. The people needed to be able to think clearly when the morning finally came. Emeth escorted Irena to her chambers to wish her goodnight and blessings for tomorrow's battle, as I walked with Theo, pretending to be off to my chambers to sleep as well. Before we made it there, I quickly turned and headed off to my usual place. I was sure I would be restless through the entire night and that it was pointless to even try to sleep with all the thoughts I had on my mind. I went through the passageway leading into Irena's room and listened through the wall. I still heard Emeth's voice on the other side. He was asking, close to begging, Irena.

"Any powers you still hold over me must be let go."

"I can't!" Irena said unhappily, "If I release the powers I have over you, your years will catch up to you all at once, and you shall slowly die over the next few days. I am not ready to let you go, Emeth. I can't!"

He replied, "Child, I have lived a long prosperous life. I have had the honor of knowing you and watching you grow into the beautiful young woman you have become. I have witnessed your meek spirit and kind, gentle heart. That's all your father ever wanted, for you to grow up to be a beautiful, kind lady who would rule her people. I've taught you everything your father has asked of me. You need all of your powers intact for tomorrow, including the ones you hold over me. I release them back to you and have the pleasure dying, knowing you may live."

"Emeth, no," she said in a low whisper.

"I followed you my entire life and I have never asked for anything in return; my allegiance lies with you. I never wanted to live as long as I have, but it was your choice, and I knew you needed me, until now. I believe you can be just fine on your own. I am an old feeble man, useless to you and unable to help in any way during the battle tomorrow. I can offer you nothing. You must let me go. I give you permission to take back what is meant to be yours. We must all die eventually Irena, but your time is far ahead of you."

With a heavy heart Irena lifted her hands over Emeth and gained her full powers and strength, what was keeping him alive. He fell to one knee from weakness and she cried.

"I'm alright my dear. I just need to lie down." The guards escorted Emeth to his chambers. Before leaving he told her not to worry about him. He promised her he wouldn't die until she returned from tomorrow's battle. He promised her he would see her again one last time. Irena quietly shut the door behind him and shrunk to the floor, weeping. I came in and went over to her, down beside her and holding her in my arms. She cried on my shoulder for a few minutes until she calmed down.

We both knew we had only about five hours to spend together, so we took advantage of our time. I noticed sketches of the tower where Irena and I had visited on her desk.

I asked her about them, "Something about this tower gives me the chills."

"Yes, I cannot get the visions out of my head so I drew it. I suppose that is where it will end.'

We spoke of the new memories we had made in the new city of Avalon, of the new friends we now had, and of our relationship. After a couple hours talking and holding each other tight, I kissed her as if it would be the last time I would ever kiss her. We spent another half hour looking into one another's eyes until we eventually drifted off to sleep in each other's arms. We were awoken by the guards outside of the door. Irena was to be the last one woken when everyone else was ready. Our army was waiting outside on the horses. This was it; the day I would always remember, good or bad. Whatever happened on this day would be the biggest moment in my life. I looked out the window into the dark of the night while Irena dressed behind her trifold screen. A mannequin held her armory. It was gorgeous gold armory fit for a queen and it was hard to imagine Irena ever having to use it. When she was decent I helped to fit the rest of the pieces onto her.

"I have to go get ready myself," I told her.

She turned to look at me and said, "This may be the last time we are together." I bent down to kiss her again.

"I'm going to keep you safe my darling." I said.

"You mustn't interfere," she said back.

"What good would I be to live a thousand years without you?" I questioned her, and she smiled back at me. There was a knocking at the door. It was her servant maids.

"Just a moment," Irena said as she walked me over to my way out.

"One more thing." I paused. "The ring you have on your finger? I'm guessing I gave it to you once upon a time. If you will still have me, and we make it through this day alive, would you do me the honor of marrying me?"

She shouted "YES," and slightly covered her mouth for fear someone might have heard. We exchanged our love vows again and I was gone, leaving her standing there, excited and happy. It was just the way I liked to see her. Maybe for a second we both forgot the situation we were in. I was happy to have distracted Irena, if even for a moment. We were content with the time we had spent together and I was grateful for it. Back in my chambers Theo had heard the news of his grandfather.

"He will be alright until we return," I tried to reassure him.

"If we return," he said.

Outside the men were ready. I thought of my father for a moment. He crossed my mind as I looked around at all of our strong men. This must have been how he felt when he left me for war. What a glorious morning we had ahead of us. I went to get Mecarth. I decided not to feed him this morning hoping that maybe he would be more aggressive against our enemies. I put his harness on him and we rose up into the sky, about fifty feet off the ground. We circled above the soldiers down below.

From up above, it was the first time I was able to see all of our soldiers together at one time. Our numbers were outstanding, in the thousands. I felt better about the war looking at all of the fierce men ready for battle. Finally the queen arrived on the scene and glanced up at me before she held out her sword in front of her and led all of her soldiers marching forward. They followed at a steady pace behind her. We only had a few miles of distance to ride. It started to rain and we could barely see ahead, especially from my view above. Flying was even more difficult. I had never flown Mecarth in the rain before. He didn't particularly like it either. Theo was with the first row, almost right beside Irena. I knew he would do all he could to keep her safe. I hoped he would also watch his back as sometimes he got a little too brave and reckless. One wrong move was all it would take and the outcome could be costly.

16. The Great War

When we finally arrived to the battlefield Irena had envisioned, there were no other troops to be seen. I landed Mecarth on top of a large stone to keep my eyes on Irena.

"What is it Irena? Why have we stopped? There's no one here," I yelled to her.

"Not yet, but soon, when the rain stops. Get ready!" She commanded. I held onto Mecarth and waited with the rest. The rain stopped and the men looked around at each other for a second, amazed by the Queens prediction. She never stopped staring into the distance. I looked forward and could see movement ahead. The dark army's armor was black; it blended in well with the trees across the field. They had been traveling for weeks, most likely without any stops. One after another they came out onto the open field marching toward us. The army was well organized and struck terror in our army. Our men were anxious to strike as the soldiers grew closer.

"Not yet," she said to them. After a while, as many more gruesome soldiers headed toward us, Damion appeared from the brush. He was riding on the back of a black stallion. It was hard to imagine now that I used to be among the few trapped men in that same army, so many lost souls. The way I felt about life now was so different from those days. I almost felt sympathy for them. I pitied them in a way.

Damion had no respect for royals in battle. There was no line up, horns blown, or flags waved. Every single one of them came at us with everything they had. Closer and closer from across the field we watched and waited until Irena gave the signal and we attacked forward. It was just barely morning and the air was thickly humid. Irena rode alongside of her men into the crowded battle ahead. Theo fired as many arrows as possible in the enemy's way, taking them down one by one. There were already wounded soldiers from both sides struck down. I flew Mecarth closer to the ground and he grabbed many soldiers, taking them up into the air and throwing them back down. We flew past all of the fighting and he blew fire into a crowd of soldiers running onto the battle field. I looked back to see what was happening with Irena and Theo. Damion looked surprised to see me with Mecarth and, infuriated, he used his powers to shoot his own fire balls at us. Mecarth was quick, dodging each one and then spitting fire back at him. Damion then used his powers to make a giant line of fire on the battlefield, striking down anyone in the way. Irena was close to the line and put out some of the fire with her own power. Mecarth kept taking them down until we rode far enough to see the end of his army. From up high it looked hopeless; there were more from the dark army swarming in on us. No one could see past the trees at how many were coming at us, but I had flown past the trees and hills and looked off into the distance as the very last soldiers were running toward us. The view was terrifying. Thousands of men from each side would die here on this day.

If we destroyed Damion, maybe his army would draw back and retreat. It was easier for Mecarth to attack our enemies when they weren't so close together. We rode through the hills and took out as many soldiers as we could see, not taking very long. Mecarth was very fast. I turned quickly to head back and help Irena. Flying back into the main fighting area I saw an enemy try to strike Irena's horse down and Theo stuck him with an arrow. Right after this happened an enemy archer shot at Theo and got him right below his shoulder. Theo let out a gasp of pain, but kept on shooting. I had to help him. It was time for back up. Mecarth let out a roar that was to signal our surprise attack. Most of Damion's army was already on the field by now. Agrius led the rest of our men from each side, trapping the enemy in the middle, defenseless.

They couldn't see our men hiding in the surrounded trees until it was too late. Agrius and his men were good at blending in with the forest. Most of our backups were mystical creatures. By this time Damion was agitated and maybe a little worried for his own army. This was such a waste, all this death. It sickened me. I flew down to help Theo, not wanting him to get hurt anymore than he already was.

"I'm fine," he said to me.

"You get on Mecarth and he will take you back to Avalon," I ordered him.

"We're not finished yet!" he yelled at me.

"Theo, that's an order. You're wounded and there's nothing else you can do!" I helped him onto Mecarth, unsure of how my dragon would take it. No one else had ever ridden him before, but it was worth the risk.

"How's are numbers? Do you think we won?" he asked me.

"I'm not sure yet. Where's Irena?" I looked in every direction and did not see her anywhere.

"She was just right here," Theo said. I had to find her.

"I'll shoot from the air until I run out of arrows, then I'll return to Avalon." Theo rose up into the sky so I couldn't argue. I fought beside Agrius.

"Have you seen Irena?" I let out a gasp. He, too was, unsure where she had disappeared to. He noticed Damion was missing as well. Theo yelled to me from the sky, "Alick," and he pointed over to the castle ruins. I could see Damion and Irena standing, facing each other in a courtyard. It would take me a while to make it through the fighting to get to her. I pushed my way through. Agrius covered me. A great light shot out from the courtyard and I could not see what was happening. The light stopped for a second and I saw Damion pushed onto a stone column. The light started again, this time brighter. When the light stopped again, Irena was kneeling on the ground, but then stood back up. She was weakening, but still strong. They had each struck each other once. She handled what he was throwing at her and fought back even harder. They kept shooting their powers at one another as they made their way up the tall tower steps. I was finally able to reach the courtyard. Then Callum stepped in my way.

"Move aside Callum," I said. He swung his sword at me again and again.

"What stops the queen from loving me if you're dead?"

For a second he almost had me and then an arrow went through his neck from above. Theo had his bow drawn and started pulling back. 'Thank God,' I thought. It must have been his last arrow. I had to hurry. With my sword drawn, I made my way up the winding staircase and headed in the direction I last saw Irena and Damion go. I know Irena asked me not to interfere, but I couldn't just sit back and do nothing. I had to make sure she was alright. On the way up to the tower, I checked every door that I passed by to make sure they weren't in any of the rooms. I listened for any sound, but they were all empty.

Light filled the sky once more. 'Higher,' I thought as I kept climbing the stairs around the tower. I opened the last door and behind it they were both there staring at each other, hands lifted and waiting for the other's next move. The room was large, dusty, and had stone columns all around it holding up the walls. They both saw me enter at the same time and looked back at each other ready, planning their next moves. They both looked drained, as if they were running out of energy, but they were relentless. Both of them could take a serious hit. Damion's face was unrecognizable to me. He was a lot older than I was and not what I was expecting. I imagined him a lot younger, and yet, he was starting to have grey hair.

"Ah, if it isn't Alick. So nice to see you again. Do you even remember me? Or anyone for that matter?" He started laughing. "It's been some time since I last saw you. When was it? Oh yes, it was when I sent you through an empty portal. How in the world did you manage to get back here? You must've died."

"Leave her alone and fight me. You hide behind your powers," I said.

"It would be my pleasure to kill you again." He quickly lifted one hand at me and shot his weapon of light at me. I ducked behind the nearest column. He missed, but destroyed most of the stone column above me; some pieces fell on top of me and I covered my head with my arms to protect myself. My face was scratched up and my leg was caught under some stone. At the same time, Irena shot at him. With the other hand he had lifted to her block her powers, he had struck her as well and she fell back. "This really was all too easy," he said looking down at her. She tried to stand back up. He had barely shot her, she screamed in agony. My leg finally came undone and I ran over, swinging my sword at him. He met my sword with his. We quarreled clashing our swords together several times. Our battle carried us out of the room, continuing up the tower steps, leaving Irena to recover and regain her strength.

I wondered how long I could keep this up before he got bored and started using his powers again. Irena needed a break and, at the rate she was going, I wasn't sure if she could last much longer. To the very top of the tower we continued fighting. There was only a tight space for moving around. We circled around the room, hoping I would buy Irena more time. He would swing and I would duck. It wasn't long until our blades grazed each other. I hit his chest, but the armor protected him. He pinned my arm with the tip of his blade and once again on my leg. I kept swinging and missing until I sliced him on his side below his ribs. After my strike he rammed his powers in me for a few seconds until I was lying on the floor, unable to fight any longer. It was like I had been struck by lightning. Coughing, unable to breathe normally, I tried to say something. He raised his blade in front of my face. "Tell me, do I still haunt your nightmares? Stay here for me. I'll come back for you after she's dead." Damion started for the door. It took all I had to grab him, almost tripping him. He turned and kicked me in the head, leaving me unconscious.

My head was pounding, my eyes were flashing from the trickery of the lights. I could hear my own breathing, feel my unending pain. I stood up and leaned against the wall. I tried to hurry, but my leg had a limp. I hadn't the slightest clue how long I had been out. I could feel my heart beat pulsing through my entire body. Limping down the stairs, I could see the door ahead. I feared the worst. Irena had to be dead; I had taken too long. My life would be over if she had died. I imagined I would end my own life to forget the pain of losing her. I heard voices coming from inside. I heard Damion say, "There is no hope for you." I knew I had heard that phrase somewhere before. Light flashed out from the doorway, and I went in, watching with astonishment. Irena was shooting the brightest light I had ever seen into Damion. Damion was fighting back and also fighting off a younger version of me who stuck a blade deep into his stomach. Irena's light ran out and Damion struck her for a split second and cast his last energy into the man who looked like me beside him. Irena fell to the floor. Damion was hit by her last bolt which sent both men to the ground. I remembered this scene from before. Yes, I was from the past and traveled through the portal to the future. I remembered finding Irena and kissing her, telling her it would be alright, and fighting Damion. I rememberd shoving the blade into him, and then dying shortly after. I hurried over to all of the bodies lying around on the ground. I first saw myself; eyes open, dead, facing Irena. The last image I remembered seeing; her lying on the floor, still. I limped over to her. Damion was still breathing.

"How did you?" He was gasping for air. I looked down at him and said,

"When you sent me through the portal, guess where you sent me?"

With his last breath he asked, "Is she dead?" I raised my sword and shoved it through his heart. 'You are,' I thought. His body disintegrated from the evil that resided inside him. 'It's over!' I thought.

17. A Birth of Peace

I turned to see my worst fear, her lifeless body with no sign of movement. I dropped down beside her. My hands were over her shoulders as I tried to shake her awake. I began to whimper as I realized she wasn't breathing and a part of me died looking at her. I wrapped myself over her body and held her tight.

"Come back to me," I said to her, "You can't leave me," I wept. My memories came back slowly until I had every single memory that we had ever made together, flashing before my eyes. "Please," I begged again and then I kissed her on her lips as my tears fell onto her cheek. I could feel her breathing lightly again. I looked at her and her eyes began to patter open. That familiar spark, I felt it again running through our bodies together.

"Alick," she said in a low whisper.

"Shh, it's me my darling; it's really me, and I'm here. Don't say anything. You'll be alright. You did it Irena, Damion is gone forever. You won!" About half an hour later, Irena's strength was restored, although she lacked her powers. I helped her to her feet and then we made our way down the tower steps, wondering how the battle was going on outside. When we appeared in sight, hundreds of our men were waiting on us and cheering. Agrius ran over and told us that we had won the war. We couldn't believe it. His dark army could no longer feel his presence and retreated. They rounded up and captured many of Damion's men. Agrius informed us that all of the injured soldiers would remain in the dungeon as our prisoners until they received their final judgment from the queen.

"Release them," she urged.

"Your majesty?" Agrius questioned.

"Do it. Let them know we aim for peace. Let them return to their lands and families if they have them. Let it be known from this day forward that the war is over and Avalon has won. Anyone who is against us will suffer the highest punishment, death. We will form a new world of peace beyond our own lands. Everything will change." Agrius nodded and tore the rope free that was tied around the prisoner's wrists. The prisoners were confused. They had never been shown mercy before and quickly ran away into the forest.

"Are you sure they deserved to be set free, Irena?" I asked her.

"They can no longer do any more harm here; their leader is dead," she told me and I agreed with her. We watched our enemies disappear and hoped that, when the years passed by, we wouldn't regret our decision to let them go.

When we returned to Avalon, Theo greeted us. His arm was wrapped up in a cloth. The examiners had already pulled out the arrow and treated his wound. Irena was thoroughly examined and returned afterwards to visit with Emeth. Theo told us that while we were away, he had also visited Emeth and finally confessed his sins to his grandfather, who forgave him. Irena visited him that day and, days later after his passing, she told me about her last conversation with him. She told him that she was unsure of how she'd survived. Emeth guessed that since her powers had always strengthened when I was near her, he thought since there were two of me in that room when she died, that her powers were more vibrant and, she came back to life. Now she had another chance. Emeth almost didn't believe her story about my old self coming through the portal to the future from that ship. Emeth also guessed that with Irena's powers, she could only travel to the past through the portals. When they experimented with the portals trying to figure out how they worked, Irena could only go back in time and was back in the body of her old self. With what Theo told Emeth, he figured, Damion's powers only let him travel to the present and that was how Theo could see him. So when Irena and Damion's powers combined on that ship, it somehow shot me to the future through the portal and I was still in my same body. He guessed that was what had happened to me. It was my portal travel that ended up saving us all. It was unknown, even to Damion that someone could travel to the future. Now we understood properly how the portals worked. There were ancient portals left all around the world. Irena had one of her own, but still feared there was much that was still unknown about them and decided it was best if they were left alone. Emeth passed away the very next evening and he was buried next to the old body of Alick. We buried the body of my old self and the past with it. We hoped this would be a new beginning. All of the bad could be put behind us. Irena and I finally learned how to live a normal life together, worry free, and we had each other again. We never reflected much on what had happened in the tower that last day, only remembering what could happen to people when they were forced to make a tough decision or tempted with something evil. It was humanity's greatest flaw, following others. It was the saddest part of our being.

Something about the following months felt differently to me, happier even. There was change in the air. The city felt refreshed and stronger. We were finally at peace. Irena had done what everyone had always believed she would to do. Now she could do what she was always truly meant for; she ruled. We married that next spring. Years passed without any sign of Irena's powers returning, and she grew older, but not as fast as everyone else. So did I. Our purpose had been served. I was sure with her powers weakening that mine were too and I was no longer immortal. Maybe it happened when I saved her or when we said our marriage vows; maybe I had no more lives left to live. Our people were safe and happy and that was all that mattered to us. Mecarth was set free, but stayed near the castle of his own free will. Theo learned from his mistakes and met a lovely girl and settled down. Agrius traveled home, and Irena and I visited him from time to time. I remained his close friend for the rest of my life. I can still remember some of my best days and memories that were made over the next few years. For nine months I impatiently waited for my precious baby girl to be born. I thought my wedding day was the happiest day of my life until the day when I held her in my arms. During Irena's pregnancy her stomach would glow every now and then, mostly when the baby would move around and kick. Irena and I worried about it for several months, wondering what it could mean. We sought out answers from fairies. They told us it was good power. Finally a beautiful baby girl was born and we named her Alina. Perhaps it was possible that Irena had passed all of her powers and immortality down to our daughter. The city celebrated our daughter's arrival for three days. We could tell she was special like Irena from the beginning, and her name suited her well. Alina meant light. She was possibly stronger than Irena had ever been, even as a young child. I could see her mother's strength in her. She had the same blonde hair and rosy cheeks. One day, when Alina was only a toddler, I walked her through our castle gardens. The gardens grew taller with her presence. Alina could make a flower path wherever she walked. I saw goodness in her. Alina's powers were so wondrous that the fairies decided to stay and watch over her. Neither I nor Irena worried about her upbringing because she was different, or what the future could be like for her with magic. I never wanted her to have to fight for what she had, or run because someone else wanted to take it from her.

When she was older, Irena and I decided it was time to travel back to our countryside to the old Avalon and rebuild and fill the city with joy again. We formed a new city. Alina's life was just beginning. Alina had her own destiny to fulfill. And I can say that, like most stories, Irena and I lived out the rest of our days happily ever after.

Return to Avalon
(An Epilogue)

Stepping on the shore was a relief. We had been traveling out at sea for weeks; finally reaching our destination. Home. Irena was delighted. Alina was the age of four and I remember putting her little feet in the stern ground of sand beneath me and following her track of foot prints not far from behind her. The wind blew through Irena's hair and I pushed it aside from her face. All of our ships arrived not long after ours. The lost people started cheering for our permanent arrival of stay. After everything was unloaded from the docks I kept my girls down at the beach for a little while longer. I wasn't ready to return to the city just yet. I wanted to soak in the first day back with no interference. For hours Irena and I played with Alina. I told her the story of how I met her mother on a shore not too far from this one. This beach was very similar. There were tall cliffs around us and many rocks for Alina to climb. This would be our secret place to escape; filled with privacy.

Alina was much like her mother in many ways. Not only in her beauty as much as her mind. She was tender hearted and very observant. I looked from her to Irena and she smiled slightly back at me. Then I bent down to kiss her forehead softly and she began to freely run around in circles with playful laughter. The sun began to set with a vibrant ray of orange in the sky. Alina's eyes reflected the light. I could stare into them forever. She had cast a spell onto me; a father's unending love. She could do no wrong. I sat down with Irena to watch her play as the day was almost to an end. She picked up various sea shells and brought them over to show us; like her mother did when she was only a child.

I looked down at the last one that she had put in my hand. To my surprise it looked very similar to the one I had once given Irena for her collection. I opened my hand to show her. She kissed my cheek.

"I promised I would find one of these for you again someday. I never imagined it would be our daughter that would find it for me."

This was our future. I never expected something so good for myself. Irena didn't need to speak for me to know by the look in her eyes that she was looking forward to the days to come. This was a new feeling that we could both get used to. We felt very blessed. It was like we had been given a second chance. Irena leaned on my shoulder as we walked slowly back to the city.

"Daddy, daddy."

Alina jumped into my arms.

I couldn't help but to think of the time Irena jumped into her father's arms. The memory made me appreciate this moment even more.

I would like to thank Chad Williams for the editing. Without your refinement, this story may still be unfinished. Lori Shultis, thank you for the image designs and making my visions of characters come to life on paper. To my children Preston, Jenna, Ali, Summer, and Chloe who make my imagination grow stronger each day and inspire me to make believe. And to my husband, Edwin, for always believing in me and encouraging me to follow my dreams.

Photo by Rachel Wright Samonia Portraits

Lauren Jeffares Parra wrote ***Protecting Avalon***
after an inspiring dream she had of the main characters. She is
working on making her work available as a series. She wrote an essay
in High School that was ranked top five best out of her graduating
class. She is also a photographer and lives with her husband and small
children in Smyrna, GA.

laurenjparra@yahoo.com